A PROFESSOR'S

REVISED EDITION

DONALD F. AVERILL

ISBN 978-1-966540-66-3 (softcover)
ISBN 978-1-966540-67-0 (ebook)

This book is a work of fiction. Names, characters, places, and incidents are the product of the author's imagination or are used fictitiously. Any resemblance to actual locales, events, or persons, living or dead, is purely coincidental.

Printed in the United States of America.

INK START MEDIA
265 Eastchester Dr Ste 133 #102
High Point NC 27262

A PROFESSOR'S

REVISED EDITION

DONALD F. AVERILL

CHAPTER 1

SEPTEMBER STIRRED and began to move her arms and legs slightly as she awakened. The soft blanket extended to her neck, but her nose and ears were cold. She couldn't understand why her feet felt cold too, for they were under at least several layers of bedding. She wiggled her toes; they were cold, just as if she had been playing in snow for hours when she was a child and the freezing temperature had penetrated her rubber boots, shoes and soaked her socks.

She barely opened one eye to survey the bedroom, the other buried in her pillow. The box of tissues was beyond her reach and her pillow was turned sideways; things were not like her organized room at home. She sniffed her runny nose and glanced at the digital clock, the ticking synchronized with her heartbeat; an odd time was displayed: 68. The alarm should have buzzed at 7:00 a.m., but it hadn't sounded; was it too early, or had she been sleeping so soundly it didn't rouse her? September couldn't remember arriving at the cabin in the mountains of Oregon, coming in, and getting in bed, so maybe she was mistaken. She couldn't understand why her memory was so fuzzy.

She thought Von must have carried her in from the car and put her to bed. It wouldn't have been much trouble for him; he was six-two, weighed over 200 pounds, and was built like he still played college football. She had probably drifted off in the car and was so deeply asleep she didn't wake up when they reached their mountain home. She was very tired, even after sleeping what she thought must have been at least eight hours. It couldn't have been past midnight when they arrived, they had been approaching the cabin before it became dark.

Von came in the bedroom, bent over her, and kissed her forehead.

"I think you have a little fever, Nine."

She sighed, "I'm wondering why I feel so tired."

"Well, maybe it's a combination of the cold and the change of altitude," suggested Von. "I think you need something to eat. You haven't eaten since we had snacks yesterday afternoon."

"But I don't feel hungry, I just feel tired." She glanced up at Von and said, "How is Honey?"

"She's fine. She's asleep on the floor in front of the fireplace. She wandered around the cabin early this morning and checked everything out while I built a fire. Typical dog activities; sniffing everything." Von smiled. "I'll get you something to eat, whether you want it or not. You should nibble on something—be right back."

Von returned to the bedroom in a few minutes carrying a serving tray with toast, grape jam, and some apple juice.

"Von, could you please close the curtains? I've got a terrible headache. The light hurts my eyes."

He pulled the black curtains closed. "It quit snowing and the sun came out. Icicles are rapidly melting." Von went in the bathroom and returned with a large bath towel to use if she became nauseated. He unfolded the dark towel next to her pillow and grinned, "Just in case."

September looked at the food but had little desire to eat. She assumed a white pill on the tray must be aspirin. She swallowed the tablet and took a little sip of apple juice, leaned back against her pillow and closed her eyes. The darkness was comforting, she had no sensory input but that from her fifty-four-year-old brain.

Von was at the bedroom door. "I'll be in the lab. Use the intercom if you need anything. Hope you feel better."

September went back to sleep but was awakened by a loud whirring noise coming from the roof. She reached over to the nightstand and pressed the intercom button.

"Von, could you please see what is making the noise on the roof?"

"Okay, hon, just a minute. I'll check."

In a few minutes the metallic sound of the front entry latch could be heard, followed by the thud of the heavy wooden door shutting. Von appeared in the hallway and leaned into the bedroom.

"There was a woodpecker tapping on one of the roof vents. I threw a small snowball and it flew away." Von frowned, "How's your headache?"

"It seems a little better now. Thanks for taking care of the noise."

"Okay. Go ahead and get some more sleep; it'll do you good. I see you took the aspirin." He smiled as if he had cured a deadly disease.

September was drifting away from the confines of the cabin, but occasionally stirring and glancing around. After about thirty minutes, full consciousness returned, but she worried that the headache would come back. She slowly peeled back the layers of blankets. It was still light outside, but dim in the bedroom, so she realized she couldn't have been dozing very long. She sat up in bed and ate a piece of dried toast and sipped a little warm juice.

Dizziness forced her to sit on the edge of the mattress and get used to being released from the pillows and covers. Five minutes elapsed before she stood up and went to the bathroom, touching the walls for support and guidance. After freshening up, she removed her gown, put on some clothes, and went to see Von and Honey. She held the dark stairway railing tightly as she descended the dozen steps to the living room hardwood floor.

Von and the dog were in the dimly illuminated laboratory at the end of the shadowy hallway. Von was looking at something with his microscope and Honey was sitting nearby watching from the shadows. September entered the lab and asked, "Why is it so dark in here?" Both Von and Honey looked up at her as if her appearance had been unexpected.

"I only need the microscope light, dear."

Honey got up, tail wagging, and walked slowly to September.

"Hello, Honey!"

September reached down and scratched the dog's head.

"How are you feeling, Nine?" Von asked, concern showing on his face.

"Much better. I'm getting my land-legs back but I'm still a little dizzy. Do you think we could go for a short walk? I'd like some fresh air. The cabin is a bit stuffy; don't you think? It's not dark yet, is it?"

"Sure, we can do that; it's only three o'clock. There's still another ninety minutes of daylight. Let's get some of that fresh mountain air. The snow has nearly all melted except for a few spots in the shade of the trees and cabin." Von flipped off the microscope lamp and got up from his lab stool in near darkness. "We'd better wear jackets. I'll get Honey's leash."

Outside, they walked a short distance on one of the paths leading into the woods. Beneath the layer of pine needles, the path was still firm and slightly overgrown with grass and unruly weeds, leaving a walkway only a foot wide in most places. September noticed the large variety of pinecones, randomly scattered on the forest floor, in all different shades of gray and brown, some almost black. She gathered a few cones of different sizes and picked some small light-brown ones to fill her jacket pockets. September looked into the forest and up to the sky. "Why is it so dark? It isn't very late."

"The canopy shades us and it's very cloudy today. Have you some ideas for the pinecones?" Von asked.

"Uh-huh. They'll be part of Christmas decorations."

Honey was pulling on the leash so Von followed the dog about twenty yards off the path into the trees. The dog wanted to go farther into the woods but Von thought better; he pulled on the leash and Honey returned to his side.

"Von! Quit throwing things at me!" yelled September.

"I'm not!" Von shouted back. "Cones are falling from the trees. Did you get hit?"

"Almost. I'm sorry, I thought you were fooling around and tossed one at me. I think I'd better go back. I'm not feeling very well; my headache is returning."

"Okay." Von addressed the dog, "Come with us, Honey. We're going back to the cabin."

Von grabbed September's arm to steady her and they made their way to the cabin with September's harvest of small pinecones. After they removed their jackets, September placed her pinecones on the island countertop in the kitchen. Von laid a few pine boughs beside the cones.

"Where did you get those?"

"When Honey went off the path, I cut them from a couple of small trees—from limbs within easy reach."

September raised the cuttings to her nose. "Umm, they smell wonderful. I've got a magazine with an article about pinecone and pine bough decorations. I'll see if I can find it."

"All right. While you work on your decorations and after I add some more logs to the fire, I'm going back to the lab. Yell if you need anything."

Honey followed September into the bedroom where September sat on the bed and began looking through a stack of magazines. She was unable to find the article she wanted. Her headache was getting more intense than before. She pushed the magazines aside, leaned back against the pillows, relaxed, and fell asleep. Honey jumped on the bed and curled up beside her during the search.

About an hour went by before September heard Von's voice. "I wondered where you were, Honey. You've been watching over September, haven't you?"

September felt Von's hand touch her forehead. Her eyes opened and she looked up at him.

"Oh! I guess I fell asleep again."

She sat up, yawned, stretched her arms, and looked around. She gathered the periodicals and set the stack on the floor; the article was somewhere else.

"Von, did you see that man?" she asked.

"What man?"

"Hmm, maybe I was dreaming. There was this man and a big black dog—even bigger than Honey. The man wore a black jacket and there was a watch in his pocket. I could see the chain. His hair was very long."

"Boy, that was a pretty vivid dream," stated Von. He joked, "Did you talk to him?"

"No. I saw him from the bedroom window."

"Huh, I didn't notice. I thought the curtains were closed. Would you like some dinner, Nine?"

"I'd like chicken soup and soda crackers, and maybe some tea with one sugar cube." She smiled, "My headache is gone."

"Your command is my wish, Madame," Von replied with a grin at his joke.

"While you are in the kitchen, I'm going to check the weather on TV. I'll be by the fireplace." She picked up the remote, stood by the fire, turned on the TV and tried to scan through the channels. She tossed the control on the sofa. "Von, the TV doesn't work. I can't get any programs; everything is black."

"That's odd. Give me a second, I'll try the set in here."

The kitchen TV didn't work either and the radio couldn't pick up any stations. He tried to call the contractor on his cell phone, but there was no connection to Hugh.

"Boy, this is really strange. We can't get signals of any kind. I'll have to ask Hugh if he had any trouble like this when he was building the cabin."

As soon as the soup was hot, Von took a tray to the living room, put up a card table and they had dinner by the fire. As they ate, they talked about the lack of contact with the outside world. After the soup and crackers, September sipped tea and Von had coffee. Dessert was chocolate ice cream.

September was curious, "Could the solar array on the roof be blocking the phone signals?"

Von replied, "I don't think so, but I'll go outside and try again," He returned after a couple of minutes. "The damn phone doesn't work, Nine. There must be something wrong with the satellite."

September shivered. The loss of contact with the outside world reminded her of the TV show *The Twilight Zone*. "Oh well, let's watch a movie. I'll make some popcorn."

After watching an old western black-and-white love story, Von went to finish some things in the lab, then checked Honey's food and water. September had retired but was sitting up against her pillows reading a magazine.

As Von came into the bedroom, September said, "Hey, I found the article about using pinecones and boughs for decorations."

"I bet you'll create some beautiful things. We can hang one of your wreaths on the front door." Von continued, "I finished my lab project and Honey is asleep in her bed by the fireplace. I'll drive back to the clinic in the morning and see if there is anything urgent. Give me a list of your needs. I'll get them and come back in the afternoon."

"I've got all I need right here. Honey and I will keep busy with pinecones and cuttings. Oh, yes, there is something. Could you pick up some ribbon for me? I need red, green and gold, about an inch wide, but not wrapping ribbon, cloth ribbon from a fabric store."

"Okay. I've got your order."

Von reached over and turned out the light; then he turned to September and gave her a good night kiss.

"G'night. I'm almost finished reading."

Von had already gone to sleep when September finished her article. She turned out her reading light and slid under the covers.

CHAPTER 2

WHEN THE new day sun arrived, Von let Honey out and September started coffee. As she added water to the coffee maker, she glanced out the kitchen window. Honey was sitting in front of a big, shaggy, black dog. It looked as if Honey were listening to advice or instructions being given from a trail guide.

"Von, Honey is out with an enormous black dog. Could you please check on her?"

"You mean the dog from your dream?" Von quizzed.

"I don't know, but there's a large black dog out there with Honey right now."

Von went out and called Honey. She turned away from the dreaded canine and slowly walked to Von and sat down. The odd creature turned and bounded through the grass and thorn-riddled blackberry shrubs into the woods.

Von reached down and scratched Honey's head. "You're all right, aren't you girl?"

Honey stood, wagged her tail and followed Von into the cabin.

As he unzipped his gray jacket, Von said, "Honey's okay, she would have barked if there were any danger, don't you think?"

September thought for a moment. "I guess so, but that dog looked threatening. It was just like the one in my dream. I wonder where the owner is."

After breakfast, Von went out and checked the car. He started the engine and returned to the cabin to don a heavier coat.

"Boy, it's pretty nippy out there." He moved to the kitchen. "If I leave now, I'll get to the clinic about ten thirty. After lunch, I'll pick up your ribbon and should be back by around four p.m."

"Make sure you check the phones and find out about the TV reception. Okay?"

He smiled, "I'll do it, boss."

As he went toward the door, he gave September a kiss and said, "Stay warm and work on your decorations. That'll keep your mind active. There's more firewood right outside the back door. I sure wish I had the week off."

"Thank you, dear. See you at four o'clock."

As Von opened the door, Honey ran between his legs and went outside.

"I'll let her back in the cabin in a few minutes—after you're gone," stated September.

Von got in the car and gradually pulled away from the cabin.

September was watching as Von leisurely drove down the dirt access road. She watched Honey run after Von and get in the car. She smiled, turned away from the window and walked over to the pile of pinecones. She looked at the cones and boughs and said, "It's just you and me, guys."

September retrieved the craft magazine from the bedroom, placed it on the kitchen counter, took three pencils and a drawing pad from the top drawer of her writing desk and sat on a bar stool. "What else do I need?" She thought for a moment, placed the big ceramic cookie jar within easy reach, took a deep breath, exhaled, and was ready for creativity to strike.

Designs for several decorations of pine boughs and cones flowed from her pencils as the hours slipped by until time for lunch. While cleaning off her work area, she saw a man when she glanced out the kitchen window. He resembled the man in her dream, dressed in black. She watched as he walked slowly past the cabin on the path she and Von had taken the day before.

He appeared to be about sixty but she couldn't see his face clearly. If it was the same man she had noticed before, he had gotten his hair trimmed. She ran to the front window and saw him follow the only worn path and disappear from sight into the forest. He walked like a much younger man than one six decades of age.

Before September returned to her design work, she loaded the CD player with Christmas music. Although it was seven months before Christmas, she wanted the mood to help catalyze her imagination. As she worked on her designs, she made a list of different size pinecones she needed. Another hour passed before her supply of cones that made her designs come to life was exhausted. She had to go outside for more.

When Von returned with the ribbon, she could liven up the dark sections of her designs with splashes of red, green and gold. She wished she had asked him to get some spray on snow but she could do that later. Silver glitter would be useful, too.

She donned her heavy coat and looked out the front window to see if the transient was still in the vicinity. Just in case there was any problem, she put pepper spray in her pocket and picked up a knife from the kitchen. She intended to cut more boughs for her artwork, but it crossed her mind that the knife would also be a good defensive weapon. Honey left with Von so she wouldn't have her dog's protection, but Honey might not be much help anyway; she was too friendly with strangers.

Outside, and after locking the front door, she turned and went down the path in the opposite direction the man in black had gone. She saw no reason to encourage a possible confrontation and neither Von nor Honey were around for help. She walked to the edge of the clearing and found some small noble firs where she could get some cuttings. As she removed a few small boughs from the diminutive trees, she reflected on how these little trees might look as Christmas trees. A quick decision was made; she would never cut down any of the small trees.

September retrieved a plastic sack from her pocket, placed several of the cuttings in the bag, and crouched down to pick up a few pinecones near her feet. They were the perfect size. As she rose, she heard a noise from behind. Startled, she spun around, dropping the bag and knife. She reached in her pocket for the pepper spray and scanned the ground to locate the paring blade.

The man in black didn't move. "I'm sorry, ma'am. I didn't mean to frighten you."

It was the man she had seen earlier. He was about six feet tall and had neatly combed shiny charcoal hair; his facial features looked as if they had been chiseled from stone. He appeared to be a Native American. Dressed entirely in black, he was an intimidating figure.

"Oh! You frightened me." She looked into his jet-black searching eyes. "Who are you?"

"My name is Revo Hctaw," he answered monotonically without any expression, his dark eyes focused on her face. "It's an Indian name that was given to me by my mother. She occasionally spoke to the Great Father. My name is pronounced hawk-ta but it is written h-c-t-a-w. Mother believed there were too many vowels in the English language. She left out the unnecessary letters. I am what you would call a caretaker."

"I'm September Hilliard."

"Yes, I know."

"You're a caretaker? Did my husband hire you?" September asked.

"You might say that."

"Where's your big dog?"

"Rover's around somewhere. He comes and goes—visits with the animals in the woods. He's kind of an animal psychologist and goes where he's needed. I believe he talked to your dog, Honey, earlier today."

"I like that—the dogs talking to each other," September smiled. "So, where do you live, Revo?"

"I've got a temporary place about a mile from here, adjacent to a small creek."

"A tepee?" September laughed, then followed with, "No disrespect meant."

He also laughed, "Don't worry about that. I lived in a wigwam once. I'm from Maine. Nope, never had a tepee. It's an RV with all the conveniences. I painted a wigwam on the side of it. I'll probably be here for most of the summer and then move to the Midwest or East when the need arises. It all depends on things beyond my control."

"Well, I'd better get back to the cabin. I've got work to do before Von comes back. It was nice meeting you."

"Nice meeting you, September. You take care."

September watched Revo walk off into the pine trees but he did not follow a path. She turned, picked up her knife and plastic bag, and made her way back to the cabin. The music was still playing when she unlocked the door and went inside. After securing the door, she emptied the bag on the counter and thought about her talk with Revo. Concern for her safety had almost vanished—Revo appeared to be a very nice man and since Von had hired him, she had nothing to fear.

September got busy with her newly acquired materials and assembled several of her decorations. The ribbon would provide the finishing touches. She looked at the clock in the kitchen. It read 4:12 p.m. The microwave, the stove, and the coffee maker clocks all indicated 4:12. She thought Von must have synchronized them before he left. Sometimes he took care of every last detail. He was an endocrinologist but acted like a surgeon.

At 4:30 she began to get a bit concerned. Von had said he would be back at 4:00 p.m. He must have had to stay at the hospital to take care of an emergency. At 5:00 p.m. September realized Von wouldn't drive up to the cabin in the dark so she decided not to worry. Neither the State Patrol nor Park Rangers had come to the cabin, so she knew Von was all right. Surely, he would come back in the morning. Of course, the mountain roads were susceptible to mud and rockslides and downed trees could block the roads at any time. That could take a couple of days to clear. She would have to be patient.

September was suddenly awakened at 4:12 a.m. Brief flashes of illumination, apparently from lightning, penetrated the dark bedroom curtains. The occasional bursts of bright light were enough to cause September to wish Von had returned from Portland. There wasn't even a rumble of thunder, the noises of the storm had been silenced by the trees surrounding the cabin and the great distance of the lightning. She drifted off to sleep and was reawakened at 8:00 a.m. by the rapping of the front door knocker.

She put on her robe and slippers and went to the front entrance, but she glanced through the peep hole to see who was there before she opened the door. It was Revo, he had returned. She unlocked the door and opened it a shoe width with her foot as a door stop. Revo said, "Good morning September. Is everything all right?"

"Good morning, Revo. Everything is fine here. Did the storm bother you?"

"The wind rocked my RV a little bit, but that was all."

"Would you like to come in for some fresh coffee? I'm going to make some right now."

"Thank you. I would like that. My early morning coffee was reheated."

September turned on the coffee maker and sat down on one of the bar stools.

Revo had followed her into the kitchen and pointed at the Christmas decorations on the kitchen island.

"Did you make these?" he asked.

"Yes. I assembled them after we talked yesterday."

"You do beautiful work."

"Thank you. Von's buying some ribbon for highlights—to add a little splash of color."

September filled two mugs with coffee, opened the cookie jar and put some molasses cookies on a plate next to Revo.

"Black coffee and cookies! A great way to start the day," stated Revo as he smiled briefly.

"Revo, does your cell phone work?"

He shook his head, "Don't have one."

"What about your TV and radio?"

"Don't have those either."

"How do you keep in touch with the world?"

"I communicate with nature. That's all I need. Nature has a pulse of its own."

They sat quietly for a few minutes, enjoying the coffee and cookies. Revo finished his coffee, took another cookie for the road and left the cabin.

"Bye Revo. Thanks for stopping."

"Bye September. Thanks for the refreshments. You take care."

September watched Revo disappear into the woods. He walked as if his feet hardly touched the earth. Rover hadn't made an appearance. She dressed quickly and took two large pinecones to the laboratory. She was determined to see if she could discover if there was any medical benefit from pinecones. She spent the morning applying chemical tests to pinecone scales.

When it was about time for lunch, Von had not returned yet; she would have another meal alone. She reasoned that he must have been delayed at the hospital. Following a quick lunch, she put on some classical music and went back to work in the lab. The next time she looked at the clock, it read 4:12 p.m. She thought that time seemed very strange; it kept popping up. She thought she should enter the lottery and use numbers 4 and 12 as two of the choices or maybe 41 and 2. The investigation of the compounds she could isolate from the cone scales continued until after dinnertime. She kept putting off dinner thinking Von would arrive, but it was nearly 8:00 p.m. and Von had not returned.

She called it quits for the day, turned off the equipment and went to the kitchen. The small TV in the kitchen wasn't working, but the appliances were. She went to the freezer, picked out a frozen dinner and popped it in the microwave. The chicken teriyaki wasn't enough, so a scoop of ice cream and some decaf coffee completed her dinner. She had decided to stay away from caffeine; she didn't want to wake up at 4:12 a.m. again. A full night's sleep should remove any remaining cobwebs from her mind. After cleaning up the kitchen, she went to bed thinking about Von not showing up as planned. September yawned, put down the operation manual for the centrifuge and turned out the light. It was almost midnight.

In the morning, Revo returned to see if September was okay. She was already up and dressed when he arrived. September opened the door before Revo had a chance to use the knocker. She had seen him approaching the cabin.

"Good morning, Revo."

"You surprised me. Good morning. How are you today?"

"I'm just fine, thanks. Would you like some fresh coffee?"

"No, thank you. I've got some business to tend to about a mile from here. A hunter needs me. I would like a cookie though."

"Just a sec. I'll get you some cookies."

September went to the kitchen and put three large cookies in a Ziploc bag and returned to the front door. She handed the bag to Revo.

"Thank you September. They are very good cookies. I may not see you again for a long time."

"Are you going away?" September asked.

"No, but Von might be back soon. I won't be needed then."

"Oh! Have you talked with him?"

"No, but I have a feeling."

"Thank you for checking on me, Revo. Goodbye."

"Take care, September."

Revo turned, walked away from the cabin and disappeared into the woods. He didn't seem to walk, he just kind of floated, but his legs moved like regular walking. She wondered if that was typical of Native Americans. He was the only one she had ever met.

For the first time, September thought Revo was a little bit different. He sometimes almost talked in riddles. It was as if he were in touch with another spirit. He was caught up in tending to the needs of others. But he appeared to be a simple man, generous and thoughtful, much like a nurse or perhaps an angel, but weren't they always dressed in white?

September closed and locked the door. She turned on some music and went to the lab to continue her studies of the pinecones. As September worked, she began to miss Von more than ever. It would be so nice to have him helping with her investigation. Von was always encouraging her in whatever she ventured. He wouldn't hesitate to show her the best way to get chemical information from the pinecones. She admired the confidence that he displayed when working in the lab.

She heard some muffled noises almost like bells. Could that be Von? She put down the scalpel and ran to look out the front window. The SUV was coming slowly toward the cabin and she could hear the beeping of the horn. It was Von! She ran to the door and unlocked it.

CHAPTER 3

MY NAME is Nedrik Miles Curtis: BA mathematics, Washington State University. I stood a few millimeters over six feet, wore glasses, and had short brown hair back then. Now, almost fifty years later, my hair is slowly turning gray and getting thinner, especially on top; male pattern baldness is creeping across the crown of my head. I'm beginning to look like my father when he was in his sixties. An old friend from high school once called me by my father's name.

Thinking back to the summer of 1972—it was unusually hot in Moscow, Idaho, not far from the St. Joe National Forest. So, during the day I studied on the front porch of the cottage I was renting. The covered wooden porch extended across the front of my rental. I didn't have air-conditioning, few people did, but erratic soft breezes were stirring the air. The scent of the forests added a little spice to the beauty of the university campus. I was trying to memorize a table of geologic periods when three children came running across my front yard, yelling and jeering. The skinny little girl fell down and the two boys chasing were laughing, pointing at her, and yelling, "Dummy!" I stood up so the boys could see me. Surprised by my presence, they turned and ran off in the direction from which they had come.

"Are you all right?" I asked the girl as I walked across the porch in her direction.

She was on her knees, wiping the dust from her bare, scratched arms. She looked up at me. "I'm okay, mister. I tripped on a stupid weed. Don't you have any grass?"

I grinned, "There's some out in the backyard. I'm saving on water. I'm just renting; I don't own the place. The landlord supposedly takes care of the lawn—or the weeds in this case. What's your name?"

"I'm not s'posed to talk to strangers. I'm on my way home." She stood up, turned, went down three steps to the sidewalk and slowly moseyed down the street, occasionally skipping.

I thought she looked a little scrawny for an eight-year-old. I was guessing her age. She disappeared into the house at 225. My address was 215 E. Maiden Lane, just two houses away. Whoever she lived with must have recently moved in; that was the first time I had seen her. I had been at 215 for nearly two years. The house at 225 was also a rental, a little run down, usually occupied by college students during the academic year, but this was June and most classes were out for the summer. I thought 225 was vacant.

The second time I saw the young neighborhood girl was at the mom and pop grocery store about two blocks from my cottage. I was out of wieners, hamburger, and lunch meat, so I was buying staples for lunches and dinners for a typical graduate student. I carried a plastic basket and had started filling it with a loaf of whole wheat bread and a package of buns. I rounded the aisle heading for the meat counter when I saw my neighbor girl. I think she was with her mother. Their hair was the same color and they both were of the same body type; they were thin—looked a bit malnourished. They were standing together at the checkout.

"I didn't see the aluminum foil. I'd like a roll." The woman accompanying the girl was talking to the cashier.

"Aisle five, between the frypans and storage containers." The cashier didn't look up; she had the store merchandise committed to memory. "You must have missed the sign—foil is listed. Have the girl get a roll for you; it's in a new package made by Alcoa: pink and silver."

The mother spoke to her daughter, "It's on aisle five, Willa." She pointed to aisle five. Willa walked in the right direction, but went one aisle too far, to aisle six. It appeared to me she didn't understand the aisle numbers. I was six feet away from the aisle, so I said, "Willa, it's over here," and pointed. Now I knew the girl's name: Willa.

I understood the confused look on her face; she was getting too much information and wasn't able to sort it out. I walked down the aisle with her and pulled a package of foil off the shelf, handed it to her and smiled, "Here you go."

Willa hadn't recognized me from a few days ago when she had fallen in my front yard. Perhaps it was due to the change of environment. I've done that before; when someone passes you on the street and says hello, but you don't know who they are; like a bank teller but not behind a counter. Willa looked at me as if I were a total stranger, but suddenly a light flashed on and she grinned, "Oh, you're the man on the porch. Thanks!" She bounded off to the cash register carrying the aluminum foil in both hands. I hoped to see that grin again. She was cute when she grinned. I wondered what her laugh was like.

While I walked home with my two bags of groceries, I began to analyze the actions of the little girl. By the time I got home, I had two major questions: could she read and did she perhaps have dyslexia? I had only recently learned about dyslexia when I was taking teaching classes. I was certified to teach secondary school math and science. I wondered where she had been going to school, if she had ever been in school. It occurred to me that the two boys chasing her might have been teasing her about her inability to read, but I was only guessing. Next time I see her, I'll sneak some pertinent questions into our conversation, if I can get her to talk to me. Perhaps I'm no longer a stranger.

I was consumed with my summer job for the next ten days and didn't see Willa. I got a job working with the civil engineers in Pullman, ten miles west of Moscow, at the highway test track. They hired me as a mathematician and I was making enough money to pay for another year of graduate school, as long as I didn't squander any money on frivolous activities. Unfortunately for me, dating was one of those activities.

I had to earn the best grades possible so I could maintain a teaching assistantship. My math degree hadn't prepared me for geology classes, so I was saddled with undergraduate geology courses to prove to the department that I deserved financial assistance. I had a week off from working at the test track because part of the track was being reconstructed and no data was being generated. That week was devoted to my new field of study: geology. It had been nearly three weeks since I had seen Willa.

A couple more days passed and then I saw Willa in her front yard. I hoped she would come by so I could practice my detective routine. I was on the porch again and the wind chime was playing a five tone sonata with no perceptual beat. I was able to think clearly with the pleasant background sounds from the chime the only thing I could hear. I found that unusual, because I usually liked studying in silence—nothing to detract from my thoughts. I was reviewing some geologic terminology when I heard a girl's voice.

"Hey, mister. Whatcha doin'?"

I glanced up from my book and saw Willa dragging a jump rope behind her.

"I'm studying. Where have you been for the last few weeks? I haven't seen you around."

"We went to the mountains to see my dad."

I had an idea about her father's activities; I would have bet that he was panning for gold. There was still some low level amounts of the precious metal in the nearby forests.

"So, you were camping by some streams?"

"We lived in a tent beside a creek. I got a little sunburned." She pulled down the neck of her T-shirt and showed me the slight sunburn on her neck and shoulders. "I was fishing—for trout."

"Catch anything?"

She nodded and said, "I got a big one about this big." She held her hands about a foot apart.

"Did you eat it?"

"Nope, we let it go. I caught two others, but they were too small—like little goldfish. I let them go, too." Her eyes drifted to my book. She pointed, "What's in that book?"

I felt I was making some headway; she wanted to know about the book! I held up the book so she could see the orange and blue cover, and the large white letters spelling geology. The entire title was *Geology of North America*, but all I wanted was the first word.

"Do you know what geology is about?"

She shook her head but seemed to be interested. She was curious about my book.

"Geology is the science about the history and structure of the earth. I'll bet your dad knows some geology. Gold miners know a lot about geology."

That comment caused some alarm and she became uneasy. She dug the toe of her right shoe into the dirt and looked away from me. She rubbed her hands on her tattered jeans.

"I have to go." Willa turned and walked quickly—almost ran across the weeds and tufts of grass to her house.

Ten minutes later, the woman that I had seen with Willa at the store came charging up the walk to my porch. She was scowling and I knew I was in for a tongue lashing, but I wasn't sure what it would be about. Would it be for talking with her daughter or for guessing that Willa's father was a gold miner? Those were the only things that struck my mind.

"I want you to quit talking to Willa. I don't want you putting ideas into her head. She already has enough problems. Please leave her alone."

"I'm glad you came over. I'm Ned Curtiss, a graduate student. I taught high school a couple of years ago and I noticed your daughter might have some difficulty reading. I was trained to watch for such things." I took the steps down to the walk where Willa's mother was standing. We shook hands and the angry frown began to melt.

"I'm Helen Walker, Willa's mother. Will you please do as I asked?" The sour frown had returned, but less pronounced.

"All right, but I would like to help if you would let me. I might be able to help her overcome some learning problems she might have at school."

"She doesn't go to public school; I'm home schooling her. She was being teased, so I took her out of public school. We're doing just fine without your help." With those statements, she turned and walked stiffly down the sidewalk.

As she walked away, I said, "It was nice meeting you, Mrs. Walker." I couldn't see any reason to get testy or sarcastic; I was serious. I felt like Mrs. Walker was not well informed about dyslexia and didn't have the patience or knowledge to help her daughter. I decided to keep out of the storm's way for the present, but I hadn't given up hope. I wanted to help Willa. I knew what it was like to be teased at school.

About a week later, on July 4th, I went to the city park, only four blocks from my house, to watch the neighborhood fireworks. It was Saturday, so the families would probably be out in full force. I went early, when I could still see where I was going, and found a seat on a small knoll near the tennis courts. There was a sign giving instructions for the pyromaniacs to follow for safety. The last time I had taken part in lighting fuses was about ten years earlier when I was fourteen, a freshman in high school. Back then I suffered a numb hand when a firecracker went off in my fingers. It didn't cause any permanent damage but I learned to be more careful; some fuses were faster than others.

I took my geology text with me so I could study while there was light enough to read. To catch up with my classmates, geology majors, I had to make use of every minute for cramming. I looked up occasionally and watched entire families plop down on blankets to watch the pyrotechnics. I knew it wouldn't be too long before the display started when I saw the city fire engine and four firemen begin supervising the people carrying bags of mortars, rockets, Roman candles, punks, and matches. Firecrackers, even lady fingers, weren't allowed.

I thought I heard my little neighbor's voice above the hubbub and turned my head to the left. About fifteen yards away were Willa, her mom, and I presumed, her dad, sitting on a colorful blanket. Willa was carrying on with her father in a very animated way. She stood, turned toward me and waved. I waved back and she came running over to my grassy mound.

"Are you here all by yourself?" she asked.

"Yep. Just me and my book." I held up my geology text.

"Where's your girlfriend?"

I smiled and said, "Don't have one." Then, with no thinking at all, I said, "You want to be my girlfriend?" As soon as I had blurted out those few words, I realized I had made a mistake, even though my utterance had been in jest.

"I think you're too old and I'm too young to have a boyfriend."

"Yeah, I guess you're right. I don't have any money to spend on girls anyway."

"Well, I came over to ask you to join us. My dad wants to meet you. I told him I didn't know your name."

"It's Ned Curtis, Willa." I stood and said, "I'd like to join you and your parents. Thanks for the invitation."

Willa did a quick about-face and waited for me to follow her to the family blanket. I looked down at this waif-like girl and reached for her hand, but she was already moving. Just as well, that could have been an even bigger mistake. Willa was at the family blanket four or five steps before I arrived. Her father was standing and extending his hand.

"I'm Ben Walker. I believe you know my wife and daughter." We shook hands and I answered with, "Ned Curtis. Glad to meet you. I met your wife and Willa several days ago."

"Have a seat, Ned."

Ben's hands were rough but he had a strong grip, not unexpected for a man panning or sluicing for gold. I wondered if he had tried his wife's moisturizer on his rough hands. I almost grinned but held back. I nodded to his wife and sat down beside Willa, but not too close. My left knee popped when I dropped to the ground.

Willa giggled, and said, "Firecracker!" She had a cute laugh, about what I expected from an eight-year-old.

"Willa!" Her mother scolded.

"That's all right," I said, "I thought it was funny, too," and grinned.

Ben was about five-nine and well-built; he could have been a boxer. He was wearing a tight-fitting T-shirt and his biceps were bulging from his shirt sleeves. If he wanted, he could probably beat the crap out of me with ease. I had to watch what I said, there was no need to rile a tiger. His hair was long and sun-bleached, the roots dark brown. He looked like a hippie but he came across as a down-to-earth hard worker. He had to be if he was going to make a living panning for precious metal. Gold mining was a rough job, but from what I heard, finding nuggets was exciting.

I thought for a minute and then asked, "What is gold worth these days?"

There was a pause, but not long, and he said, "A little over thirty-nine bucks an ounce."

There was another pause and then he followed with, "Willa told me you had figured I was panning in the mountains."

"It was just a lucky guess, but I knew most of the activity in the mountains around here was based on searching for gold. About a year ago a friend of mine showed me a map of claims. He was going to spend a few weeks investigating—but he never did. George was killed in a plane crash. I never found out the exact reason, but it was determined to be accidental."

"Sorry you lost a friend, especially at such a young age."

"Thanks. We weren't close. We had taken a few courses together. We were classmates."

The first mortar lit gave a loud thumping sound and a few seconds later the sky flashed with an explosion of silver sparks and red streaks in a spherical shape. The burst echoed across the city and there was a chorus of oohs and aahs from the onlookers. The celebration continued for the next half-hour and came to an end when most all the children were given sparklers. The tennis court lights came on and the firemen began picking up the spent mortars, etc., and hosed off the asphalt surface. A nearly full fifty-five gallon drum containing all the used devices was loaded on the firetruck for disposal.

CHAPTER 4

I WALKED HOME with the Walker family. Upon arriving at Willa's house, I was surprised by Ben's offer. We hadn't talked much during the time at the park.

"Mr. Curtis, how would you like to help me on my claim for a couple of days? You can keep half of what you find."

"Thanks for the offer, but I have some classes I can't afford to miss. But I'll think about it. When can I let you know?"

"I'll be going back in the mountains on Monday—you've got about thirty-three hours." He smiled. It wasn't an ultimatum; it was just a fact. He could only spend the weekend away from his claim. Claim jumpers were a common problem in the forests. There was too little law for assistance.

"Thanks for the offer. I'd like to do that. I'll let you know tomorrow afternoon. I need to consult with a lab instructor."

Sunday morning, about 9:30, I went to the geology lab, about a half mile trek, and found my Tuesday lab instructor in his office. Tod Baxter was slaving away on his doctorate and was usually in the geology building 24/7. When I knocked on the research lab door, he invited me in and asked how he could help me. I explained what I had planned with my neighbor for Monday and Tuesday. He listened attentively and told me I could come to the Thursday lab session instead of my regular Tuesday lab. He thought a couple of days panning for gold would be good experience for a geology student. I returned to my cottage by way of the Walkers' and told Ben it was a go. He asked me to be ready at 5:00 a.m. tomorrow and bring at least one change of clothes and boots; make sure I had a pair of boots.

I didn't have a duffle bag for my things, but I owned a large suitcase and a mailing box for sending home dirty laundry. As an undergraduate, I'd sent home shirts and underwear for my mom to wash and return the clean clothes. I think she wanted to keep in contact with me more than ensure that I was wearing clean underwear. I didn't write many letters home, but I'd stick a note in with my dirty things. I always found a note from Mom in the box when I received my laundered clothing. She also included some homemade cookies—usually a half dozen, oatmeal.

I chose the box rather than the suitcase, packed it with some clothes, my geology book, and a spiral-bound notebook. I almost forgot something to write with, but at the last minute, I tossed in a couple of cheap ball-point pens. I wouldn't have a pencil sharpener out in the wilds.

I later thought that I could sharpen pencils with my pocketknife. I sat in the living room going over the things I needed and recalled Ben had told me I needed a pair of rubber boots which I didn't possess. I recalled my landlord telling me I could use anything in the garage so I looked around in boxes and cabinets and discovered a pair of waders. Mr. Saunders was a fly fisherman. Fortunately, the waders fit perfectly. Confident that I was ready for the mountains, I went to bed about 10:30.

My alarm was set for 4:00 a.m. and I shot out of bed when it went off. For some reason, I thought someone was at my front door. I sat on the bed rubbing my eyes and laughed; I didn't have a doorbell. I shut off the alarm, pulled on my pants, and stood there looking around and then relaxed, sat on the bed and put on socks and shoes. I didn't bother to shower. I ate two eggs, scrambled, and two pieces of toast decorated with low-calorie grape jelly. I skipped coffee and drank about four ounces of milk from the quart carton. I put on my light jacket and sat watching the clock for about ten minutes. Just before leaving the house, I made sure the furnace was off. I laughed at myself again; the furnace hadn't been on since the end of April, according to Mr. Saunders.

I locked my cottage door at 4:51 and walked over to the Walkers'. Ben was sitting in his beat-up old Ford pickup waiting at the curb. It was still dark, but the corner streetlight was bright enough so I could see the cracks in the concrete sidewalk. The truck windows were down and he said, "Morning, Ned. Toss your stuff in back and climb in."

I followed directions, slammed the door, and we roared off. I was thinking he didn't have a muffler when he commented, "I high centered and lost the muffler last Friday."

"I guess the roads are pretty rough where your claim is."

"Yeah. We have to make our own way to get in and out with our equipment. Too much stuff to carry very far."

We drove about half an hour before leaving the main road, and then another forty-five minutes or so on a gravel road that wound around the increasingly steep and rugged forested hills. The sun was coming up but we were in the shade until we left the graded surface. The roller-coaster ride to the claim took another ten minutes of white knuckles. We suddenly stopped and Ben announced, "We are at Camp Walker."

Ben had chosen the site wisely, about thirty feet from the water; a stream about twenty-five feet wide. The tent hadn't needed any poles, it was supported by a tree branch, eight feet up and parallel to the ground. Ropes to stakes pounded into the ground supported the tent walls, about four feet high. I was guessing it would sleep a dozen if the kitchen were not present. A small pot-bellied stove sat in one corner, waiting to be fed kindling, pinecones and small dry branches to keep the tent warm at night and provide a cooktop.

"Put your things in that corner, slip into those waders, and I'll put you to work. The summer work will keep my family going for another year." He pointed to the bare corner of the tent, apparently where Helen and Willa would be if they were visiting. I saw an air mattress rolled up and hanging from a hook dangling from the tent wall.

I dropped my few belongings and slipped on the waders. I found Ben at his sluice box checking to see if it was damaged. Apparently not, after the inspection, he stepped off about twenty feet along the bank and opened a diverter. Water from the creek began flowing down a channel, through the box, and back into the stream. He joined me and gave me instructions so I could work alone. Then he picked up a large shallow pan, scooped up some silt on the bank, and began to process the sample of dirt and pebbles.

I waded out ten feet with a large pail and shovel. Downstream from a large rock, I loaded debris into the bucket. I let it sink about six inches into the water and filled it with more material. When full, I lugged the pail to the sluice and dumped it onto the half-inch sieve. I poured water over the debris on the sieve and washed the small material onto the sluice and discarded the larger rocks after checking for nuggets. No nuggets—just as I expected, so I went back for more material. I lost count after more than ten shovelfuls of rock and sand had been carried to the sluice.

When my hands and feet were so cold I was losing feeling in them, I took a break and sat on the bank watching the ripples in the water as it flowed by on its way to the Snake. The sun was out now and felt really good, almost therapeutic, on my aching back and arms. My prune-like fingers were beginning to warm up when Ben joined me.

He smiled, "Not that much fun, huh?"

"I didn't expect it to be fun, sir, but I didn't think my hands and feet would get so cold so soon."

"You've done fine, Ned. Damn near ninety minutes is more than most men can stand before warming up. That suns feels good, don't it?"

"Sure does. When will we clean the rugs in the sluice?"

Ben sucked on his lower lip a bit and then said, "We'll wash 'em after we have some lunch—about one o'clock."

I had moved my watch above my elbow so it wouldn't get wet and I glanced at the face.

Ten-thirty meant I was going to freeze my hands and feet for another two hours, assuming we'd have thirty minutes for lunch. I didn't want to show any signs of weakness or being a wuss, so I got up and went back to work. I wanted to earn as much respect from Mr. Walker as I could before asking him about Willa's education. In fact, as I walked back into the stream, I decided to wait until the second day before I asked Ben if Willa could read. My education courses had informed me that all the necessary tools for reading should be in place by the end of the second grade. At the ripe old age of eight, Willa should be in grade two and comprehending written material.

While loading the pail and dumping it on the sluice, I tried to keep my hands out of the water as much as possible. Unfortunately, my feet were not insulated in the waders and my toes were getting frozen, or at least I felt that was the case. When Ben called, "Time for lunch," I dumped another load onto the sluice and took off the waders. The sun on my feet felt so good, I didn't want to stop the soothing heat treatment to eat. But when my stomach growled, I knew it was time to take on some fuel. I wondered what Ben, or perhaps Helen, had made us for lunch.

Coffee, ham and cheese sandwiches, celery stuffed with peanut butter, and two sugar cookies filled me up. Ben and I got to work on the rugs from the sluice box and an hour later we had recovered 1.38 ounces of gold, or about $54 worth. His panning added another quarter ounce for a total of $63.50, not bad for about four hours freezing our hands and feet.

We got back to work and spent the afternoon toiling away. As the sun warmed us up considerably, the cold water took longer to take effect. We took a break at 3:30 for a couple of cookies and coffee and some brief conversation. Mr. Walker didn't have much to say and I didn't want to be bragging about my college education, but we talked about the mountains and the animals he had seen while hunting for gold. I was impressed with the calmness he exhibited when he told me about his confrontation with a bear.

Ben didn't say much about the bear incident, just that the bear finally wandered off. I didn't pursue the matter. I wondered what I would have done under the same circumstances. Back at work, I heard whistling and determined Ben was entertaining us. When he saw me looking for the source of the whistle, he smiled, waved, and changed to another tune. He was quite good. I could hear the notes clearly over the sounds of the rushing water. I began to hum along with the whistle. Our two-man chorus performed for about fifteen minutes before we were interrupted by another miner.

Greg Denfeld was much older than Ben. I guessed he was at least in his sixties and had long scraggly gray hair and a beard to match, but he didn't smell bad. I thought that was unusual. If he had happened upon me without warning, I would have been scared shitless. But he was a kind old guy. Ben knew him because he had an adjacent claim.

When Ben introduced us, Mr. Denfeld pulled a nugget, about the size of a pencil eraser, from his work pants and held it up to the sun so I could see the sparkle and beautiful color. We talked for a few minutes, then he excused himself, and worked his way upstream along the bank around trees and boulders. He vanished about as fast as he had appeared.

Ben looked at me and commented, "Old Denfeld doesn't talk much—kind of like me. We tend to keep our thoughts to ourselves—saves embarrassment. When he finds a nugget, he comes over to show me. Doesn't happen very often."

I nodded and replied, "He seems like a nice old bird."

"Yeah. He's just living in the wrong century." Ben sighed and smiled, "Well, back to work. If you find a nugget like that, give me a holler. Where there's one, there's usually another."

"Okay, I'll let you know. Say, is this as high as the water gets?"

I was wading in one-foot-deep water but I was thinking about sampling on the downstream side of the rocks along the banks. Why should I be standing in the cold water all the time?

"No. In the early spring the runoff causes the water to be twice as high as it is now."

That was all I needed to hear, so I sloshed back to the bank near the camp and pushed my shovel into the dirt and gravel by the closest, good-sized rock I could find. That didn't require much of a search, there were five basketball size stones nearby that qualified. I chose the one nearest the water and plunged my shovel into the earth. Water seeped around the shovel and its contents. I kind of liked the sound of the rocks grinding against the metal when I dug under water; I couldn't hear very much but felt the grinding vibrations through the shovel handle.

I dumped a big shovelful on the sieve and washed the fines onto the sluice with a bucketful of water. After adding more water, I began picking off the pebbles that were on top, separated from the finer material. I was tossing marble-size rocks into the stream and added another bucket of water. That's when I was surprised. A gold nugget was staring me in the face!

"Ben! Come here! Look what I found!" My heart was trying to jump out of my chest. That nugget must weigh two ounces, that's nearly $80, in one lump!

I watched Ben drop his pan and come running. He almost fell but was able to regain his footing.

"Whatcha got, Ned?"

I pointed at the nugget on top of the sieve. "Look!"

Ben reached down and grabbed it, rolled it around in his hand and said, "That's about ten times the size of the one Greg showed us. That'll make our day. Where'd you find that sucker?"

I told him what I had been thinking and he said, "Good for you! Keep at it and we'll make enough in two days to equal a week's work, maybe two." He grinned and said, "See if you can find some more like that. Keep it in a safe place." He grinned and handed it back to me. I held it up to the sunlight to see the rich color and then shoved it in my right front pocket where I made sure there wasn't a hole. I struggled to move that big rock out of the way and kept digging and processing for another half-hour before moving to another rock and repeating the procedure.

Unfortunately, that first big nugget was the only one I found digging around three large rocks, but we got another quarter ounce when we washed the sluice rugs. We called it a day at 8:00 p.m. and had dinner. We had made $121 dollars during the afternoon and evening.

I was dog-tired and fell asleep sitting beside the campfire. Ben shook my shoulder and told me to get to bed in the tent where the mosquitoes wouldn't attack me. After having just enough energy to remove my shoes, I tipped over sideways, and was out for the night.

CHAPTER 5

I WOKE UP hearing the sizzle and smell of frying bacon. I blinked a few times and focused on Ben in his underwear standing over the little pot-bellied stove. I smiled when I saw the skillet was bigger than the top of the stove. When you're camping, you make do with what you have. I said, "Good morning." It was chilly in the woods adjacent to the cold stream water, and the little stove had not had a fire long enough to heat the tent. I pulled on my trousers, changed my undershirt, and asked, "Where do I take a dump?"

"Morning, miner. How are you feeling, a little sore?"

I stood up in the middle of the tent and stretched. That's when I felt the results of my Monday workout. My muscles were irritated and my back ached, but I'd be ready for work as soon as I got warmed up and had something to eat. I was acutely aware that my arms were still attached to my body. I wiggled my stiff fingers to limber them up, readying them for breakfast and another day of shoveling dirt, sand, and rocks.

Ben pointed at a roll of toilet paper and said, "Take the roll and arm yourself with a spade. Find a comfortable location downwind and take care of business. Deep holes are better than shallow ones." He laughed, "I don't want to step in it—my shoes are brown enough."

I hadn't seen an outhouse, but it hadn't crossed my mind until now. I hosed down a tree like a dog the day before. I found a full-service location out of the way from our paths around the camp and took care of my lower tract.

We had bacon, eggs and pancakes for breakfast. Ben had a gallon can of maple syrup that was still nearly full. I used it liberally. I wasn't worried about my blood glucose when working hard. We didn't have any butter, but that didn't bother me. While we ate, I decided to ask about Willa.

I swallowed and said, "I'm not sure how to ask this, but here goes." Ben looked up from his plate and held his fork in the air. "Can Willa read?" Ben continued chewing, loaded his fork again, and had it poised in front of his mouth.

"She's having some trouble. That's what my wife says. I wouldn't know much about it."

"Would you mind if I tried to help her? I had a teaching class about problems kids have learning and difficulty in reading was one obstacle to learning that we discussed. Lots of people have some trouble trying to read, even when they have all the tools by the end of the second grade." Ben didn't reply for nearly a minute. I waited patiently.

"My wife doesn't like people messing with Willa. Willa's had a hard time with teasing by public school kids. We took her out of first grade so Helen could home-school her. But between us men, I don't think it's working very good. Helen's not a teacher."

I remained silent as Ben finished his eggs and pancakes. After a time of quiet thought, he looked at me and said, "You think you can help her out?"

"I'd like to try. I'll have to diagnose her problems first. That might take a few days."

"You can't guarantee anything though?"

"I'm afraid not. Do you think Willa would want to try? What would your wife think?"

"I'm sure Willa would try it. She's pretty smart, but somethin's botherin' her readin'. I don't know about Helen, she's pretty protective of Willa's schoolin' and emotions."

"How about you writing me a note that says you would like me to help Willa? That way you and Helen wouldn't have an argument." Ben didn't say a thing. I finished eating.

"We'd better get back to work, Ned." Ben folded his paper plate and put it in the garbage sack. I did the same and we got to work panning and searching for more nuggets.

As I continued digging, sieving, and washing, I wondered why Ben had not answered my question about the note. Then it hit me:

Ben didn't know how to write! Some learning difficulties are hereditary and I'd bet Ben and Willa had similar problems. I wondered if he ever graduated from high school. He could have dropped out and gone to work at a young age. I figured I'd better let it go; I didn't want to embarrass him. That might eliminate any chances for me to work with Willa, but it seemed to me both Helen and Ben were interested in Willa's education.

The entire second day at the claim was about average, according to Ben. He panned and ran the sluice and I loaded hundreds of pounds of gravel, earth, and muck from around and beneath rocks in the stream. We looked at each other occasionally to see if there were any signs of tiredness but neither of us was going to give in. We worked right through lunch and in mid-afternoon, stopped for thirty minutes to snack. We finally quit for dinner at eight o'clock in the evening. The sun didn't set until nine o'clock, but we were in shade after 5:00 p.m.

Clouds were gathering but sunlight wasn't extinguished until after we had processed the rugs from the sluice. Kerosene lamps gave us enough light to function. Ben had dried the gold and was weighing the flakes on a postal scale. I sat on my blankets and watched as his eyebrows lifted when he scraped the last few flakes onto the weighing paper.

"Better than I thought, Ned. Total weight—2.28 ounces." He looked at me and smiled, "That's not quite ninety bucks."

I grinned and said, "But that's not all. I've got some more to add." I fished four small nuggets from my pocket and dropped them on the scale.

He lit up when the total weight reached 3.63 ounces. He scribbled some numbers on the back of an envelope and announced, "$141 dollars. We did good, Ned. Why'd you hold back with the nuggets?"

"I wanted to make you feel good about having me working with you. I've really enjoyed being up here slaving away for two days. I wanted to thank you for the experience."

"You don't need to thank me. I'm glad to have gotten to know you, and remember, half of what we've found is yours."

"No, you keep everything. You have a family and I already have a job at the university. I don't need the money and it was worth it to have this experience. Plus, you've fed and lodged me for two days."

He started laughing, "I hope you enjoyed the high-class accommodations—a real Motel 6. I'll take you back to Moscow in the morning. I have to get some more supplies and say hello to Helen and Willa before I come back. I'll tell Helen to let you work with Willa. I know you'll try to help her with her readin'."

"That sounds great. I've been thinking about it while I've been working. I have some ideas to try. Next time you see her after tomorrow, I hope you'll notice some improvement."

Ben got up at 6:00 a.m. and again cooked bacon. He was out of everything we would normally have for breakfast except for a half-loaf of bread. So, we had butter and bacon sandwiches and exited camp for Moscow around 7:00 a.m. The trip back home took about fifteen minutes less than it had taken us to drive to the claim. The downhill slopes and the desire to get back to his family caused Ben to be a little heavy-footed. I didn't mind, so we broke the speed limit most of the way. I wanted to get home, too, take a shower, and change into some clean clothes. I hadn't used deodorant for two days, so I knew I didn't smell anything like roses or any other flowers: more like stinkweed.

I hadn't studied a second while in the mountains and I looked forward to sticking my face in books again. I also wanted to go back to work on the test track in Pullman; it was a lot cleaner and less exhausting than gold mining but much hotter. As I was getting cleaned up, I thought as soon as I got something to eat, I would go over and talk with Mrs. Walker and Willa. I hoped Ben had discussed with Helen his desire to have me work with their daughter. If Helen didn't like the idea, my whole plan would end up in the garbage.

When I started toward the Walkers', Ben was hugging and kissing the ladies and I assumed he was heading for the grocery store. As his truck pulled away from the curb, Willa was waving and yelling, "See you on Sunday, Daddy!"

Helen was holding the front screen door open. Her light-green bathrobe was held closed at the neck and she had on a pair of fuzzy pink slippers. When she saw me, she gave me a less than enthusiastic wave, perhaps because of embarrassment, and went in the house. However, when Willa saw me, she ran up to me and said excitedly, "Mr. Curtis, are you really going to teach me to read?"

Ben had apparently made sure Helen was agreeable to having me work with Willa.

"We're going to try, Willa. You're going to have to work real hard. We'll start right after lunch—if that's all right with you."

"On your porch?"

"No, I thought we'd go to the park. Ask your mom if that's okay. Bring a tablet and two pencils, not too sharp. Can you do that?"

"Sure, Mr. Curtis."

"Remember, now. Two pencils and a tablet. Come over at one o'clock, and you can call me Ned."

"Okay, Ned. I won't forget." She started singing and skipping back home.

I went inside, sat on the living room sofa, and read my geology text for nearly an hour. I closed my book, made some fresh coffee, and sat down at the kitchen table with a pen and loose-leaf notebook. I wrote my first lesson plan for Willa.

I didn't know if Willa knew the alphabet, so that's where we would start. After that, we would move to what I thought would be useful—she would pick out the letters from various words, even though she didn't know what the words were, and tally each letter she found on a list of the letters of the alphabet. I thought this activity would be better than having her memorize words, especially since I didn't know what her abilities were. Then I planned on shifting to the sounds of the letters: consonants and vowels. I knew we might not make it through the first step, but I had some basic ideas of how to progress. After determining what she knew, I would revise my plan and adopt a new strategy if necessary.

I was going over my notes after lunch when I heard a knock on my door. It was Willa. She was trying to see into my living room through the screen door. She had her dark-brown hair in two braids and wore a yellow blouse with blue jeans. If it weren't for her cute face and braids, I would have thought she was a boy—her slim body showed little evidence of a feminine figure. I glanced at my watch; it was only 12:32. She was a half-hour early. I didn't think it would be a good idea to have her in my cottage, so I asked her to wait while I got my things. When I got to the door with my notebook and pen, it suddenly occurred to me that she might react more favorably if she liked the color of ink I was using.

"Willa, what is your favorite color?"

"Red, and then green. The others are about the same, but I like red the best."

I exchanged my black BIC pen for a four-color pen, went out, and locked the door.

"Let's go, Willa. We can talk as we walk." I grinned and she laughed.

"You're a poet." She reached out and grabbed my free hand.

Down three steps to the sidewalk, a right-hand turn, and we were off to the park. When we arrived at the corner, I asked Willa if she knew what the octagonal red sign said.

"Sure. It says cars should stop."

"That's right." I replied, but just to tell her she was correct.

That answer meant one of two things: she knew the word stop, or she knew an octagonal red sign meant stop, but she wasn't necessarily reading. I would test her and find out if she was reading what the sign said.

I discovered she couldn't read the word stop. I drew a rectangular box with the word stop in the middle and she didn't know what it said. So, I knew she had a grasp of graphical objects, and that was positive. We spent a whole hour on the alphabet and that investment showed some promise. I remembered the alphabet song and we sang it together, adding some of our own words. Willa had a knack for rhyming words. We made hand signals if the letters were round or tall, short or fat.

Fortunately, I could draw cute pictures and I told her about hieroglyphic writing on Egyptian tombs and obelisks. I had her draw me a picture and I tried to figure out what she was saying. I wasn't very good at reading her pictures or she wasn't very good at drawing them; I wasn't sure which was true, maybe a little of both. At the end of two hours, we were both worn out so we had some fun on the swings and big slide before we returned home. We agreed to meet again on Saturday because I had to work and go to some classes Thursday and Friday.

I gave her some homework so she wouldn't have two empty days without thinking about the alphabet and reading. I found out one fact: teaching Willa to read was going to be more than a simple task; we were both going to have to work at it.

As we walked home I asked Willa, "Are you tired of the letters of the alphabet?" We had spent a long time at the park engrossed in mental activities and I was afraid it might have been too much, but she surprised me with her answer.

"I never had so much fun doing school stuff. I can't hardly wait 'til Saturday. Will we come back to the park?"

"Maybe we'll work on your porch or mine. There might be too many kids at the park on Saturday. We don't need any company, do we?" She shook her head.

"I like your porch. It's higher off the ground than ours."

"Okay, then. How about ten in the morning?"

"That's all right—unless Mom has something she wants me to do."

I escorted Willa to the Walkers' front sidewalk and said, "See you Saturday."

She stood there for a moment, apparently unsure of what to do. She smiled and uttered, "Thank you," performed an abbreviated curtsy, and scampered to the porch and up to the front door.

I turned and started back to my cottage and heard the screen door bang as Willa went into her house. I felt that Willa was a little embarrassed when she said thank you. She didn't know whether I was a friend, a teacher, or an adult friend of her parents. I wasn't sure which I wanted to be long term, but right now I was her teacher.

I thought Willa had made some progress and I had learned something about myself: I shouldn't be singing in public unless I was a member of a choir. I think that was the first time I had applied the proverb that there was safety in numbers. I decided I should only sing or hum in the shower where no one would suffer from the noise.

CHAPTER 6

WILLA AND I met twice a week unless something came up that I couldn't ignore or she had some chore to do with her mother. When Willa missed one of our sessions, she always expressed her disappointment when we next met. As she began to read words from memory and sounding out new words, her new knowledge began to act as a narcotic and she couldn't get enough. Most of our missed meetings were my fault and I arranged for half-hour catch-up times in the evenings at her house. Even her mother seemed to enjoy my visitations. I was able to balance my studies, work, and my tutoring for the rest of July and all of August.

Willa was making great progress and had started to sound out more difficult, two-syllable words, and was reading slightly above first grade level. I believed that now she just had to practice. I told Helen to ask at the school to see if she could borrow first and second grade readers. If she couldn't get them from the school, she might check them out from the city library, or even go to the university library or visit the Education Department Library.

Fall classes at all schools started the first week of September. After I completed registration, I walked to the Walkers' to tell Willa I couldn't continue the tutoring, but the Walkers' house was empty. The door was open so I went in but they were gone. They hadn't left a forwarding address, so I thought I would never see my summer student again. I was going to miss her humorous comments and passion for reading. I figured I had sparked her desire to learn new things from books.

I finished my master's program in two more years and started looking for a job. I interviewed for a job at the Hanford Site north of Richland, Washington, but that didn't materialize. They hired a Ph.D. for the position I wanted. After several months of frustration, I moved to Yakima and lived with my father for several months. He was semi-retired and worked part-time for a plow company headquartered in Amarillo, Texas. I helped him set up plows at a building at an old WWII air base, worked in the orchards, and delivered radio station advertising, all jobs that didn't pay much, but kept me active.

In December of 1976, I applied for admission to the Ph.D. program in Geology at Southern Mountain State University in Colorado. I was accepted and moved there in January of 1977 when classes were to commence for the spring semester. I arrived on campus January 3. It was extremely cold and the heater in my Pinto had not worked for the last 100 miles.

I rented an apartment on the third floor of a large three-story home and was sharing the top floor with a young married couple. One Sunday afternoon, I heard a disturbance in the adjoining apartment, but after I listened closely, I realized the couple were making love and not having an argument. I had a pretty good laugh and left my apartment for an hour, giving the combatants plenty of time to cool off.

I had to make up one deficiency but was working as a teaching assistant, so grading papers and exams, supervising laboratories, and taking classes monopolized my time. I couldn't afford to fail, so I studied nearly every minute of my waking hours, except on weekends when I did my laundry at a coin-operated laundromat. I always took $3.00 in quarters for those visits. I read from a text or thought about research ideas as my clothes were being washed and dried.

I allowed myself one date per semester, but lack of funds limited what type of entertainment I could afford for two people. My dates were so much younger than I, we had little in common, and I had no idea what I would be doing once I had my doctorate. Was I going to find a job and be able to support a wife? I don't remember kissing a young woman in the four years I was working my tail off, and becoming intimate was far from a reality. In fact, I wondered why the ladies I dated wanted to go out with me, unless of course, they were just brown-nosing. I didn't consider myself very handsome, just average.

My last three semesters were devoted to research activities and my advisor and I published a research paper. Since my research was published, I didn't have to defend my thesis.

The time I would have devoted to preparing a defense was spent looking for a job and in August of 1982, I had two offers: one in Alaska and the other in California. The decision of which to take was made for me; the assistant professorship in Alaska was not funded by the state legislature. I packed my car and headed for Southern California.

Everything I owned was jammed into my light-blue Pinto and I drove to Ocean Vista, twenty-five miles north of San Diego and roughly four miles from Pacific beaches. I wondered about the name of the little college town; from the site at ground level, the ocean wasn't visible. The town fathers must have owned telescopes or high towers.

There were three members of the geology staff: the department chair, Dr. Ethan Reynolds, a full professor; Dr. Steven Telloc, associate professor; and me, Dr. Nedrik Curtis, assistant professor. We were located on the sixth, and top floor, of the science building where on clear days, the Pacific Ocean was barely visible without a telescope. I was amused that geology was on the top floor; it wouldn't have entered my mind if geology were located on the ground floor, nearer the earth's surface.

Geology was part of the Department of Physical Sciences. There were five chemists and three physicists to round out the department. The main office was on the third floor with the physics professors on floors one and two, the other floors were for chemistry. Teaching and research labs were on every floor of the building so we placed maps near the elevators and stairwells so students and visitors could find their way around. A directory on the first floor listed the professors' names and room numbers. My office was in room 614.

Mrs. Beth Arvin was the department secretary and managed half-a-dozen work-study students; most were business majors. We got along very well, sharing a similar sense of humor. I always felt I was well taken care of. It took two years of burning the midnight oil before I felt like I had a handle on things. The first summer was a blessing; I relaxed a bit and began thinking about research projects. But the second summer was a busy time repairing broken equipment. Our department had limited funding and outside technical help was a major problem; it didn't exist. Fortunately, one of the chemists, Dr. Seth Arnold, and I were able to repair almost all of our equipment.

We began acquiring some Apple computers for lab activities. Few geology programs were available and prohibitively expensive. The only computer language I knew was BASIC, but I wrote several small programs for use in the labs to augment the exercises.

My research activities blossomed during the third summer. I took some desert trips and found several iron-meteorites which I began to investigate microscopically and chemically. At the end of the third summer, I decided to try to build a scanning-tunneling microscope. The STM allows individual atoms to be 'seen', revealing the surface structure of a conductor or semiconductor. Since the atoms are smaller than visible light by three orders of magnitude, the atoms can be pictured on a computer monitor by plotting the electronic response of the microscope's probe. However, after working on the device for two summers, I had to give up. I didn't have the ability or resources to carry out the precise machining necessary. Aluminum parts didn't work, they were too heat sensitive.

During the Christmas break of my fifth year, at a department party, I had an interesting conversation with the department chairman's wife, Gloria Reynolds.

"Mr. Curtis, do you like women?"

"I sure do, Mrs. Reynolds." It didn't take much thinking to realize she was asking whether I was gay. I smiled and added, "I haven't met any ladies my age that I would want to date. The young ladies in my classes are half my age."

"Oh, I understand completely. My church group has get-togethers occasionally for people to get acquainted, would you be interested?"

I looked around the room for someone to save me from this woman, however good her intentions were. "I've never been much of a church goer, Mrs. Reynolds."

"Please call me Gloria. May I call you Ned?"

I wanted to tell her she could call me anything she liked, she was the chairman's wife, but I just said, "Please do." I smiled. It was genuine.

"Would you like to join Ethan and me and a guest for a game of bridge sometime?"

"I would like that, although I haven't played bridge since I was an undergraduate. I'm afraid I would be pretty rusty."

She smiled and touched my wrist. "That would be perfect for Ethan and me. We'd have a chance to win for a change."

"Oh, here you are, Gloria."

Professor Reynolds joined his wife, extending his arm around her waist. That's when I noticed she was about an inch taller than her husband, but she wore two-inch heels. He asked, "What are you cooking up over here, Gloria? Have you submitted our newest professor to an inquisition?"

I wasn't sure whether he was serious; he wasn't smiling, but he didn't smile often. I don't remember him ever telling a joke. I answered his question, "No, sir. Your wife was inviting me over for a game of bridge. I just have to find a partner." I wanted to be on the good side of his wife. One never knows when support might be needed for surviving the gauntlet of the university's social structure.

Gloria stepped closer; I could smell her perfume—just a hint of lilacs. She looked up at me and mouthed a thank you. She extended her hand and said, "It was so nice talking with you, Ned. We'll talk again. I'll let you know about the bridge game."

I squeezed her hand slightly and said, "It was a pleasure."

That was the first time I realized my superiors were watching me and probably the people I talked with on campus. I made a mental note to be careful. But I really didn't need to worry much; I had nothing to hide. I wasn't a member of a cult or a subversive group, and I had no religious affiliation. The only thing I had to be wary of was liberalism; I was a conservative.

Spring semester classes kept me very busy. I never did receive a call from Gloria to play bridge. The more I thought about it, the less I wanted to play cards with Reynolds. By spring break no invitation had materialized. Professor Reynolds made me uncomfortable; I never knew what he was thinking, but I liked Gloria—she was very down-to-earth. I wondered where she grew up, where her family's roots were.

During the eight day break, something interesting happened. Few students remained on campus, the majority of them spent the week at the beach, surfing, drinking, fighting and making love with people they didn't know. I, however, was able to make real progress with my research. On Wednesday, during the vacation period, I was in my office reading and falling asleep. I checked my blood glucose and it was low. I had been a type 1 diabetic for many years, having been diagnosed when I was thirteen, so ninety-nine percent of the time when I was hypoglycemic, I ate something containing sugar, drank a Pepsi or a Coke and was fine. I also carried a roll of Lifesavers in my pocket in case I wasn't near a candy or drink machine.

But this time, I got up from my lab bench and went to the end of the hall and bought a candy bar from the machine next to the elevator. I stripped the paper off the bar and walked over to the window to see if I could see the ocean, a rare sight. I took a bite of the Baby Ruth bar and leaned against the wall, looking out across the campus. I heard the elevator motor running and after at least ten seconds the bell on the elevator rang. The door opened and footsteps could be heard on the linoleum tile in the hallway. There was also a small child's voice, "Where are we going, Mommy?"

I turned to see who it was, but I was too late to see any faces. A blonde of medium height, about five-four to five-six was holding the hand of a little girl. I guessed the child was about three years old. I had no great interest in blondes, but for some reason, I wanted to see who this woman was. Perhaps it was the way she walked. I think that was what interested me; she moved with a purpose; she was on a mission. I knew I had never seen her or her child before. I lingered behind them, watching where they might be going. I was sure it wasn't my office. They passed by 614 and continued on to the end of the hall to 635.

I was right, they hadn't come to see me. The woman knocked on Professor Reynolds' door and waited, looking down and whispering to her daughter. I assumed it was her daughter, the woman didn't appear to be a babysitter. I hoped Ethan wasn't in so I could talk with this woman with the shoulder-length blonde hair, but the door opened and the mother and daughter were ushered into the chairman's office.

My office was three doors from Reynolds' on the opposite side of the hall, so I could only hear the slightest sounds of a conversation. I didn't have the nerve to stand outside Ethan's door and listen, so I left my door wide open and waited for the noise of footsteps from the hallway. I tried to read a memo concerning the availability of summer funding, but I wasn't retaining anything; the words were without meaning. My mind was garnered by a couple of glimpses of the enticing woman and child.

A pleasing feminine voice said, "Thank you, Dr. Reynolds, I think I want to major in geology. I'll enroll in Geology 251 in the fall."

Those words were very promising. If I didn't see who this woman was today, I would find out in the fall. I was slated to teach Geology 251. But the footsteps came closer and I watched nervously, waiting to see who had been to see Dr. Reynolds.

I should have been out in the hall, because as she passed my wide open door, she was looking to the right at her daughter and I couldn't see her face. I was on her left. Poor planning on my part. After the alluring figure and young child had passed my door, I walked to the hall and watched as the little girl and her mother disappeared around the corner, walking toward the elevators. Well, I'll have to be watching for the blonde five months from now. I hope the words I heard were serious; things could change by fall semester. Besides, I'll bet she's happily married.

The remaining weeks of spring semester were uneventful, but the summer was very productive. I had applied for a grant to study both stony and iron meteorites and it came through. I moved to Winslow, Arizona, to be near the Barringer meteor crater. I ended up closer to the crater than I initially thought I would be. I was hired as a part-time lecturer while I carried out isotope studies on the nickel and iron in the meteorite fragments left from the original impact that occurred many thousands of years ago. I lived in the observation building at the rim of the crater during the summer in one of four efficiency apartments. Only one other apartment was occupied—by a foreign investigator from Australia.

My summer research activities were concluding during the third week of August and I was starting to review materials for the introductory geology class I would be teaching at Ocean Vista during fall semester. I would end my summer lecture tours at the crater on Friday and drive home the day after, but I would have the whole weekend to travel if I desired. I'd still have a full week to get prepared for classes. I always hated to prepare a syllabus for a class I was teaching for the first time. It was easier to work from an old one that would only require a few changes of dates and review questions.

Thursday afternoon at one o'clock was going to be my next to last public tour and lecture. I prepared a few notes while I ate lunch, applied some deodorant, a clean shirt, and walked to the welcoming area. I was wearing my name tag as usual and tried to smile, with some success, at all the visitors. The acknowledgement smile was followed with a brief welcome to the crater.

I still got a little nervous for the talks in spite of thorough preparation. Sometimes a really stupid question would almost bring tears to my eyes, however, it was good for me to practice my patience and keep from embarrassing a visitor. I could almost always think of a sarcastic comment, but never let one vibrate my vocal cords.

As the audience began to take seats in the lecture room, I dimmed the lights about twenty-five percent, turned on the projector, which showed a welcome message and a few slides as the lights dimmed further. I glanced at the wall clock. Two minutes until the doors closed for the current session. I began scanning the audience and when I had reached the top tier of seats, a young family entered and took three of the remaining four empty padded chairs.

The man was about five foot nine and fairly nice looking, but the young woman was beautiful. Her dark hair cascaded over her shoulders and when she saw me staring at her, she smiled. The little girl sitting between her mother and father resembled the youngster I had seen months earlier when Dr. Reynolds had those two female visitors. But that was only one observation four months earlier. I didn't think anything more about it. I dimmed the lights to thirty percent and began my thirty-minute talk about the crater and its suspected origin.

CHAPTER 7

MUCH OF my public lecture had been committed to memory, so as I related the history of the crater, my eyes roved the audience and invariable scanned the young family in the back row. The pretty brunette occasionally bent down and whispered to the little girl. I imagined the youngster was bored and her mother was telling her they would go in a few minutes.

A round of applause followed the lecture's end. I always appreciated that reward, whether particularly deserved or not. There were always some off-days when the talk lacked enthusiasm. I thanked the group for their attention, turned up the lights, stepped down from the lectern, and shook a few hands. When I looked up to see the young woman and her family, they were gone. I was trying to work myself back to them as I shook hands, so I could become acquainted and discover their interest in the crater. But secretly, I wanted a close-up view of the pretty young mother. I saw no harm in that, I would undoubtedly never see the family again. Vacationers from around the United States, especially those from Texas and California, often stopped at the crater's rim to visit, use the bathrooms, and buy postcards. Typically, someone in the family was an amateur astronomer, usually a youngster.

I gathered my loose notes, dropped them in a folder, and started toward my room on the ground floor trying to rid my thoughts of that attractive woman. I saw her again when I glanced out my kitchenette window as I was making coffee. She was ushering her youngster into the back seat of an older model dark-green station wagon. I watched her circle the car quickly and get in the front passenger's seat. The Texas-licensed vehicle pulled away travelling west. I wondered where they were headed. She might be going to Hollywood; she certainly possessed the looks.

Friday was my last day at the crater. I drove into Winslow in the morning to do some shopping for new shirts and found some excellent bargains at a men's clothing store: Jenkin's Fine Apparel for Men. Fortunately, there was a sale, but even then, I spent more than I had planned; my eyes almost glazed over when I found I had depleted an entire week's pay from my checking account. As I drove back to the crater to finalize my work week, I decided the amount blown wasn't that bad if spread over a year. No more new shirts for the next fifty-two weeks.

Saturday morning, I said goodbye to the staff at the crater and hit the road. I had calculated, from distances on a map, it was about 490 miles to Ocean Vista. I set the odometer, got on Interstate 40, and was in Flagstaff forty minutes later. I headed south on Route 17 towards Phoenix and reached the bypass to Route 10 at 10:30 a.m. I stopped for a burger in Buckeye and walked around a visitor center for about fifteen minutes before I topped off the tank and pointed my red and white Pontiac towards Coachella, California, 210 miles away.

When I reached Coachella, I relaxed for nearly an hour. My butt was getting sore and my eyes were a little dry. I purchased some eye drops at a drug store and bought a snack, more gas, and consulted my roadmap at a visitor center. It took another hour to reach my apartment. My odometer read 503 miles; a little over my estimate of 490.

It felt good to be back in the university town where I knew a few people, even if they were mostly faculty. During my first five years at Ocean Vista, a couple of the science faculty had me over for dinner, but I hadn't developed many friends except for my colleagues in the Geology Department, and they were from fifteen to twenty years older. We had little in common except our interest in geology.

My apartment was on the second floor left of a quadruplex that was at right angles to another identical building. There was a large ground-level parking lot and an elliptically shaped pool, too shallow for swimming, between the two buildings. Friday night was invariably noisy when girls and booze mixed with the male tenants causing the police to arrive about midnight. Everyone scattered when the flashing red lights appeared. A few arrests were made, for under-age drinking, and I was usually able to get to sleep by 1:00 a.m. It didn't take long before

I tired of the weekend madness. I needed to find a better place to live, preferably a house in a quiet neighborhood. It was my guess that few of the partyers had Saturday morning classes, but Saturday was always a workday for me.

I used Saturdays for class and laboratory preparations, and perhaps a football game on TV, but this Saturday I was making up syllabuses. Sunday, I'd do laundry, buy groceries for the coming week, and try to squeeze in some time to watch a VHS movie rental. I hated going to a movie theater, especially when alone. Sharing popcorn with a date was part of the fun of attending a film.

I was ready for classes on Monday, checked my mailbox in the departmental office, and went down two flights of stairs to the first floor where one of the smaller amphitheater-like lecture halls was located. Full capacity of the room was eighty-eight, but I expected only about half that number in my class. The room was vacant. I was about fifteen minutes early for my ten o'clock, so I wrote my name, office number, coarse number, title of the text, and its cost—both new and used— on the slate blackboard. I had to remember to tell the students which edition of the text they needed so the syllabus could be followed without confusion. As a reminder, I wrote a note about the text on my copy of the syllabus.

As the students began coming in and finding their favorite place to sit, I watched for the blonde I had seen four months ago at Dr. Reynolds' office. There were two blondes sitting on opposite sides of the room: one was about five foot eight, tall and thin, and the other young woman looked a couple of years younger; she was short, had short curly hair and was well fed, but not fat. Neither qualified as the woman I had seen with the little girl. Since I had been watching for blondes, I had paid little attention to girls with darker shoulder-length hair. I started wondering if the blonde really wasn't a blonde at all; she might have changed her hair color since those earlier sightings. I couldn't think of a reason she would have been wearing a wig in the hot weather.

Just as I was about to introduce myself, the door opened and a pretty young woman came in and hurriedly took a seat next to the tall blonde. I looked at her closely and realized she was the woman I had been attracted to at my next-to-last meteor crater lecture. But her hair had been cut short; it was no longer the luxurious shoulder-length pageboy style I had admired. But her face was just as beautiful as before. When she looked towards me, I finished my introduction, glanced down at my notes, and started the lecture.

When the fifty minute period ended, I thanked the class for paying such close attention and commented I would see them, same time, same place, on Wednesday. I felt my lecture went well, there wasn't the usual mass exodus for the exits as I had seen in many classes before. The willowy blonde and the pretty brunette were working their way toward me as I answered a few simple questions from a couple of other students.

The blonde asked, "September and I want to know when your office hours are."

"I hope you have some office time in the early afternoon," the pretty one smiled. Then she added, "Tuesdays and Thursdays would be great—one or two o'clock?"

All I could think of was God, this young woman has everything: nice voice, beautiful facial features, and from what I could see, a great figure. No wonder she's married. But I didn't see a wedding ring.

I had to ask, "You were at the meteor crater a couple of weeks ago, weren't you?"

Her face blossomed into an enormous smile, "Yes, I was there with my daughter and husband. I didn't think you would have remembered."

I didn't know what to follow with, but I kind of blurted out, "I couldn't help noticing you." I hoped she realized I was complementing her on her looks, but I didn't want to be too forward either.

The blonde tugged at September's notebook and said, "We'll see you on Wednesday, Dr. Curtis. Oh, by the way, I'm Gail Burnett."

"It was nice meeting both of you. See you Wednesday."

I went back to my office using the elevator. It was empty so I could talk out loud to myself. "She didn't think I would remember. Huh! She must not be aware of how pretty she is." I had verified her lack of a wedding ring. "I wonder what's up with that."

The elevator pinged as it reached the sixth floor and the doors slid open. Two students gave me a funny look as I stepped out into the hallway. They must have heard my voice in the elevator, but I'm sure they weren't able to understand the words—at least I hoped that was the case. Next time, I'll keep my thoughts to myself and my mouth shut.

When I unlocked my office and stepped to my desk, I expected to see a pile of green IBM print-out sheets on my desk, but the lists of students enrolled in my classes were not there. I left my office and went down the back stairway to the main office to check my mailbox for the listings. I was surprised when I extracted my mail, it wasn't mine; Dr. Griffith's mail was in my box.

Mrs. Arvin had been watching me and said, "Dr. Curtis, your mail is on top now. I rearranged the mailboxes. Your nameplate is below the box."

"You got me, Beth! I should have checked before I grabbed the contents. When did you decide to do that?"

"Last Friday. I guess I should have warned you. Since the geologists are fairly tall, I put the geologist's mail on top; it corresponds with your offices being on the sixth floor." She smiled, "But I had some help." As I thumbed through my mail and separated the class roll sheets from the postal envelopes, Beth walked over and whispered, "Actually, Dr. Reynolds asked me to do it. We discovered Dr. Wilson from chemistry was looking through the geology department mail. Since he's short, Dr. Reynolds wanted to make it more difficult for him."

I laughed, patted her on the shoulder, and whispered back, "Good work, Beth. I wonder what his interest is in our mail."

"Thanks. I kind of liked the idea. We don't know why he's looking through other professors' mail. Dr. Reynolds thought it was a bit strange— so did I."

As I ascended the stairs to the sixth floor and my office, I glanced at the student lists, being careful to avoid tripping on the concrete steps. I didn't need a skinned shin to remind me that I had one available on each leg. The Geology 251 enrollment covered two pages. I located Gail Burnett first in the alphabetical roll and found September Howard next.

Both were listed as sophomores, but they seemed more mature than the average second-year coed. It wouldn't take me long to discover the answer to that. All I had to do was ask them Wednesday.

Tuesday started off slowly with a Physical Sciences Department meeting. We talked over objectives for the new school year and discussed which journals we would have to drop from the library holdings. The cost of journals was skyrocketing; however, our budget was fixed as it had been for about five years. We had to be careful when eliminating journals from library resources or the various scientific societies would no longer certify our programs. The next certification would occur in 1990, so we had two years to strengthen weaknesses in our programs. We needed a benefactor to supplement our library budget but there was none in sight; we hadn't resorted to saying prayers.

Following the meeting, I swung by the library and checked out some materials they were holding for me. I lugged the books and journals back to my office and dumped them on my desk in no particular reading order. The earliest I would get to them would be late afternoon. I had office hours from 1:00 to 3:00 and was to meet with my teaching assistants at 3:15; that small conference usually ran about thirty minutes. Then I would have time to review the library materials.

With the pile of reading material on my desk, I sat down and thought for a minute—just long enough to want a cup of black coffee. I plugged my mini-maker into the wall and two minutes later, I was sipping caffeine in dark-brown water. I added too much artificial sweetener and started all over. I wasted about fifteen minutes sitting there doing nothing but thinking and watching the big hand on my office clock creep up on twelve.

At eleven o'clock, I retrieved my lunch sack from my pint-sized office refrigerator and began eroding my peanut butter and low-cal jelly sandwich. As it disappeared, I jotted down some topics for the undergraduate science seminar. Taken by senior majors, there were usually from twelve to fifteen students enrolled in Physical Sciences 499, Senior Seminar. The class met on Thursdays at 10:00 a.m. I still had plenty of time to generate a list of topics before the class met for the first time.

I washed down the last of the sandwich with tepid coffee—I should have used water. After the carrot and apple were gone, I had two cookies remaining for first aid if my blood glucose level dropped significantly. Of course, there was the candy machine next to the elevator. I always carried a few quarters in my pockets just in case.

My other prep was for Minerology and Optical Crystallography, Geology 311, a five-hour course: three hours of lecture and six hours of lab per week. The first lecture was on Wednesday afternoon at 2:00 p.m. for ninety minutes and the second on Friday, same time. The labs were conducted on Tuesday and Thursday afternoons, running from 2:00 to 5:00; taught by teaching assistants with my supervision. I usually met with the lab for up to a half-hour at the beginning and when everything was going smoothly, I would withdraw to my research lab or office for some alone time. But I was always near my phone in case of an emergency in the teaching laboratory.

Tuesday morning was a flop for getting anything accomplished. Since very few Tuesday morning classes met, there was a general faculty meeting beginning at nine o'clock and extending until the president of the university ran out of dribble that had nothing to do with the sciences. Various deans introduced new professors. They received warm rounds of applause. Most of the faculty turn-over occurred in the social sciences where new liberals replaced the retirees or those that had succumbed in the last year. I rarely knew the retired or the deceased.

After the introductions, there were several announcements pertaining to the Student Union Building services and the library. When we were dismissed, I ran back to my office and took the stairs up to the sixth floor. That was my only physical activity for Tuesday. I was going to check my pulse when I sat down at my desk after the stair climb, but I never did; my thoughts shifted from the activity of my body to what occupied the top of my desk, piles of journals and multiple sheets of paper.

CHAPTER 8

I TURNED TO the article I wanted to read in one of the library loans, but it was about twelve pages long, so I took the periodical to the department office and had a work-study Xerox the study for me. A current journal was on loan for only three days, so I wouldn't have the necessary time to digest the material if I read from the monthly. I asked the student to put the copies in my mailbox and return the publication to the library. She seemed grateful to have been given the assignment. She gave me a big smile and said, "Thank you, Dr. Curtis."

Later, Beth told me the work-study students loved to get out of the science building and go across campus to the library. They usually saw someone they knew and stopped to visit, both to and from the reference collection. Beth had a hard time finding enough work to keep the students busy in her office. Most of them were clock watchers and rarely brought books to study. Beth tried to get work-study students to make better use of their time, but she had never made much progress. She found it rare for a student to follow her advice.

I had been back in my office for about ten minutes when I received a call from a textbook publisher.

"Are you Professor Ned Curtis?"

"Yes, but I'm an assistant professor, not a full professor."

"No matter. Have you considered writing a geology text?"

"That has never crossed my mind. Has someone informed you that I might want to publish a text?"

"No, sir. A short time ago we received your feedback about one of the beginning geology books we sent out for review. Your comments were very insightful and we thought you might want to submit a manuscript. You could make a very good supplement to your income with a popular text."

"Unfortunately, I have to get a research paper published in the next year or I won't receive tenure. All of my spare time has to be devoted to my research. Thanks for calling— maybe next year, or the year after. You can always call back."

"Well, thank you for taking my call. Goodbye."

"Bye."

I sat there thinking for about ten seconds and dismissed the idea of writing a text. I had more important things to consider. The next order of business was lunch, then reading research articles, and relaxing for a few minutes before office hours required that I wait for students to show up for questions and answers. I was anticipating that September and Gail might show up, but I wasn't going to hold my breath. I'd have to wait and see who came by for assistance. If nobody showed, I would be able to get some more reading done.

Lunch was out of the way and I was leaning back in my chair reading from another of the journals that had to be returned the next day. I decided the information presented wasn't useful, so I began the third journal article. I was on the last page, when I sensed someone was at my office doorway. I looked up. It was September. She was holding a notebook across her chest with both hands.

I tossed the journal on my desk and said, "Come in. Have you got a question?"

She smiled and said, "Not about the class. It's something else."

She seemed a bit self-conscious, so I said, "I can answer most questions about math, chemistry, physics, and geology. If it's something else, I probably can't help you."

"I'm sure you can help me. Do you mind if I sit?"

"Oh, I'm so sorry. I should have asked you to come in and sit down. My apologies."

I thought to myself, 'Boy, she looks great today.'

"You don't remember me, do you?"

"I remember seeing you at the crater, but your hair was much longer."

She nodded, "It was too long so I trimmed it. My friend Gail helped me. But I don't mean at the meteor crater. You met me a long time ago."

I frowned and thought back to earlier classes I had taken during my Ph.D. work, but she would have been a teenager then and in high school. "I confess, I don't remember you. I'm sorry."

"Oh, don't be sorry, I was only eight years old. I really didn't expect you to remember me—I'm Willa."

I stood up and said, "Oh, my God. You're Willa?" I couldn't believe what I had just heard. That skinny little girl grew into this beautiful young woman.

She stood and asked, "Can I give you a hug?"

Before I could answer, she turned, moved to the door, looked into the hallway, closed the door—almost shut, and walked over and threw her arms around me.

My answer came too late, but I said, "Yes, I'd like that."

I had to hug her back. I could feel the curves of her body pressed against me. I had an urge to brush her hair away from her face and kiss her, but that would have been entirely inappropriate. But those were my inner thoughts. As we stepped back, I reached for her hands and held them for a few moments. I guided her to the chair in front of my desk and she sat down. I quickly rolled my chair around to the front of my desk, sat, and asked, "How did you happen to come here to school? Tell me all about your life since Moscow. I've thought of you often."

Willa had opened her purse and grabbed a handkerchief to dab at her eyes. If I hadn't been so shocked, I would have teared up, too. I was still having a hard time believing this was that skinny little girl I helped learn to read. I wondered if this reuniting was purely accidental, designed, or fate?

For several seconds, she held the handkerchief in her hands on her lap and smiled. "We moved to Texas at night, very suddenly, so my parents could avoid paying some bills. I wasn't able to say goodbye and thank you for teaching me to read. I cried when we had to move away. What you did made a huge difference in my life. I went to public school in the third grade and have done very well in school ever since."

"Where did you move to in Texas?"

"It was a little town south of Waco called Delight. Daddy got a job with a small oil company. Oh! I have to tell you; he couldn't read either. I tried to help him, but he said he was too old to learn what children do when so young."

"You know, I suspected he didn't know how to read or write. I asked him to write a note for me to give to your mother so she would know it was all right with him if I tried to help you with reading. He told me we needed to get back to work, so I didn't force my request. He must have told your mom it would be all right with him. He didn't want you to have troubles like he had. He's a good man, Willa."

She hung her head and then looked up at me, "Yes, I loved my dad very much. He was killed in an accident two years after we moved."

"I'm so sorry. I liked working with him in the mountains. You can be proud that you had such a hard working father. He tried the best he could to provide for you and your mom. Is she still living?"

Willa nodded, "Yes. We moved to Waco after Dad died. She works for a house cleaning firm and sometimes does babysitting. Unfortunately, she smokes. I'm afraid she's going to get cancer. I've tried to get her to quit, but she doesn't seem to have the will to do it. We've argued and I won't let her smoke around my little girl."

My phone rang but I kept my eyes on Willa. I had a question about her name. The phone rang again.

"Aren't you going to answer that?"

"Not 'til after the third ring. Then I know it's a serious call." I grinned. I picked up the phone on the next ring.

"Ned Curtis here. What can I do for you?" I listened for a few seconds and hung up. "Willa, I have to go down to my lab. My teaching assistant needs some help. Can you come back Thursday? I have so much to talk to you about—lots of questions."

"I'll be back, but I might be a little late—about 1:30. I have to pick up my daughter."

"I'd like to meet your youngster. Don't worry about the time. I'll wait all afternoon if I have to. But I'll see you tomorrow in lecture. Okay?"

She nodded, stood up, grabbed her notebook, and started out the door. "Thank you, Dr. Curtis. It was nice talking with you." Willa hurried down the hall toward the elevator.

I pulled my dog-eared, annotated laboratory manual off the shelf behind my desk and left my office, locking the door behind me. I took the stairs down to the lab and asked the teaching assistant what she needed. She held up a small bottle of hydrochloric acid and said, "We're almost out of HCl. We're going to test for carbonates today. Where do I get the reagent bottles refilled?"

"I'll do it for you. The students will arrive in a few minutes. You need to be here to get them situated and warn them about working with acid. I'll take the bottles down to the chem lab and refill them. Next time, make sure you have everything you need beforehand."

"Yeah, I should have checked sooner. It won't happen again, Doctor."

"That's all right, it's the beginning of the semester. You'll catch on quickly."

The graduate assistant in charge of today's lab was Marsha McCain, a very capable student working toward a master's degree. She was about five-foot seven, had curly blonde hair, and was always nicely groomed. Although she was average looking, her personality made her quite attractive. I had seen her functioning in a help session the previous year when she worked for Dr. Reynolds. She was authoritative, possessed a great sense of humor, and seemed to enjoy teaching. She would make a superior doctoral student if she decided to take that route. I would give her a solid recommendation although I had known her for only a short time.

I put six of the small reagent bottles in a little box and hustled off to the freshman chemistry lab where I diluted some six-molar hydrochloric acid to three-molar and refilled the bottles. After delivering the reagents to Miss McCain, I returned to my office and finished reading journal articles that were pertinent to my research.

I drove away from campus a few minutes before five o'clock. A quarter pound of hamburger was cooking by ten after. I hoped I wouldn't be interrupted by a telephone call. I cooked a potato in the microwave, added a slab of butter, and a sprinkle of salt. The fried meat received a squirt of Heinz catsup and I sat down to watch the news with my partial dinner. If I didn't fall asleep during the news, I would microwave some mixed vegetables and add catsup to flavor my second course.

If I did fall asleep after the first course, I would have vegetables when I woke up, usually after a nap lasting a half-hour or so. That was my typical evening meal at home, but I varied the hamburger with chicken or salmon. I rarely ate out because of my diabetic diet. It was difficult to know what restaurants served and usually the portions were too large or the meal too expensive. Assistant professors were not loaded with money and I had to begin saving for my future retirement, even if that event was still twenty years away. I had to think ahead.

Wednesday was a repeat of Monday as far as classes were concerned. I started reviewing my class notes an hour before class started, so had plenty of time to organize my lecture. I always checked my blood glucose level before going to lecture, so I wouldn't have a hypoglycemic reaction during class. I usually ate a cookie right before lecture and put one in my shirt pocket in reserve. I washed the office cookie down with some coffee, took one last look at my notes, and descended the stairs to first floor lecture room 1A.

I picked up a piece of chalk and wrote my lecture outline on the blackboard as soon as I got to class. There were several questions before lecture so I didn't notice students arriving, but I was beginning to recognize some of the faces from Monday's group. Gail and September had occupied seats at the right center of the hall, but I only noticed Gail. Willa wasn't there.

Each time I paused to look up for questions, I scanned for Willa, but she never showed up. When class ended, I asked Gail if she had seen Willa.

"Who?"

"Mrs. Howard—September."

"What did you call her?" Gail frowned as if Willa were a foreign word she had never heard before.

"Willa. I think it's her middle name. I met her when she was eight years old—I didn't know her first name was September. That seems like an awfully long time ago."

"Oh. I didn't know that. She told me she didn't have a middle name. But we've only known each other for a couple of weeks. Maybe I misunderstood. Our husbands occasionally work together in the naval yard. Steve is a welder, and my husband, Barry, is a pipe fitter."

I was a little concerned. "I hope she's all right." I thought for a moment. "Maybe she had to take care of her daughter."

"That could be. She's been trying to find a better babysitter."

"When you see her, tell her there's a day-care center at the Education Building. It's a very professionally run facility and it's free for children of students."

"She'll love that, Dr. Curtis. I'll let her know."

"Well, I'd better get back to my office. Nice talking with you. See you Friday."

Gail gave me a smile, a finger wave, and vanished into the hallway, the heavy wooden door banging shut behind her. I gathered my notes, rode the elevator to the third floor, checked my mail in the department office, and took the stairway to the sixth floor.

I had my usual sack lunch and leaned back in my aged wicker chair by the window and thought about my research. I had to get something published by the end of the school year or my chances of gaining tenure were nil. I'd be out of a job and have to look for some other type of employment. Once dismissed from a university position, about the only place to teach would be a junior or community college. I wasn't looking forward to making that move.

Thursday morning as I was arriving on campus, I suddenly had a brainstorm. I knew what I had to do for my research paper, my floundering had been cured. Now I had to scan the literature to see if anyone had pursued my idea before. I prayed that I had come up with a new approach. However, I was going to need the cooperation from several museums in the states and maybe some foreign repositories that contained meteorites in their collections.

CHAPTER 9

MY THURSDAY morning lecture went well. My brain was tuned to the material and some very good questions from students raised my hopes about the intellectual level of the current geology majors in the minerology and crystallography class.

After lecture, I returned to my office and combed through the listings of museums that contained meteorites. As I ate my bologna sandwich and realized I had used too much mustard, I began making a list of phone numbers to call about the debris that had crashed to earth from known radiants. I had to smile when I thought my university colleagues would think I was studying astronomy rather than geology. They would have to remember that some studies in the sciences can bridge two or more disciplines. Of course, the science faculty would be aware of that.

My list of museum phone numbers kept getting longer and longer and I lost track of time. I was beginning to set up a spread sheet and organize the information when I heard a knock. It was a soft knock and when I glanced toward the open doorway, there was a child standing in the middle of the opening. For a moment, I was tongue-tied, but then I realized Willa had to be standing in the hallway out of sight behind her daughter. Even though I couldn't see her, I knew she must be there; her daughter wouldn't be alone.

"Hello, young lady. Did you come here to see me? What is your name?"

She looked at me and then looked back into the hallway. Then I heard Willa's voice whisper, "Tell the man your name, Peg."

"I'm Peggy." She stared at me and interlocked her little fingers at her waist.

Willa whispered again, "Ask the man his name, Peggy."

Peggy stepped forward as Willa moved beside her. "What's your name?"

"I'm Ned Curtis. It's nice to meet you, Peggy. I saw you with your mom and dad at the meteor crater. Do you remember?"

Peggy nodded, smiled, grabbed Willa's hand, and moved back a little bit bumping into her mother's leg. Willa guided Peggy to the chair in front of my desk, sat down and lifted Peggy onto her lap.

"Thank you for telling Gail about the children's daycare at the instructional center. She called me last night. It's going to work out perfectly."

"Hey, that's great. Gail and I missed seeing you in class yesterday."

"Gail said you asked about me. Thank you. I had a big argument with my husband. He wants me to stay home with Peggy and forget about school." A painful expression appeared as she looked at Peggy and then me. "I told him I was going to get a degree no matter what he said or did, so there was no use arguing. I recognize the value of an education, he doesn't. He thinks I should learn a trade, but I want to use my mind more than my hands."

I wasn't sure what to say except to let her know I supported her decision. "Well, let me know if I can help in any way."

"Thank you, Dr. Curtis."

"You can drop the Dr. Curtis, Willa. Should I call you Mrs. Howard?"

We both laughed at the stiffness of the proper way of addressing each other. I had always called her Willa and she had always used my first name. But now, when other people were present, we decided to refer to each other as Dr. Curtis and September, or Mrs. Howard.

It was going to take some practice to follow those designations.

I asked, "I always called you Willa. Is Willa your middle name?"

She laughed again. "No. I don't have a middle name. When I was about six or seven and kids began to tease me about not being able to read, my dad called me weeping willow when I cried because of the teasing. He said he wanted to toughen my skin. Then he called me

Willow because I was so skinny. Mom told him to quit, so he said he would call me Willa, a perfectly good name for a girl. I kind of liked the name, so it stuck until I got older and let it drop. Most of my friends don't even know about Willa."

"Oh. So, I shouldn't call you Willa?"

"No, you can call me Willa. It reminds me of how nice you were to me when I was just a kid. I've always wanted to ask you why you were so good to me."

I took a deep breath, exhaled, and said, "I was teased when I was in grade school. My ears stuck out and kids called me Dumbo and similar things because of my big ears. I would cry at home, like you did, and when I was twelve, my mom arranged for surgery to pull my ears closer to my skull. When I entered seventh grade, nobody called me Dumbo, so I guess my mom did the right thing. But my self-esteem had already been damaged. When I saw those boys teasing you, I thought I'd try to make a difference."

Willa smiled and said, "I have to confess. When you were helping me, I fell in love with you, as an eight-year-old might, and when we left suddenly, I really felt bad—not being able to say goodbye and thank you."

I nodded, "When I discovered you were gone, I thought I would never see you again, but here you are. When you told me you were Willa, I could hardly believe it. I remembered you as a skinny little girl, but now you're a beautiful young woman."

She blushed slightly. "Thank you. I wasn't sure you would remember my nickname; it was . . . gosh, that was sixteen years ago."

I grinned and said, "I have a very good memory for math and science, but not for people. You were an exception, as were your mom and dad."

Willa smiled and adjusted Peggy on her lap. "Do you want to get down?"

Peggy nodded and Willa let her slide to the floor.

I didn't have any toys in my office, but then I thought Peggy might like to play with a crystal model set—similar to Tinker toys. I pulled the box from my desk drawer and set it on the floor by Willa.

"Here's something you might like to play with." I quickly assembled a structure that resembled a dog and made a growling sound. Peggy laughed and started making something from the sticks and colored spheres.

Willa responded with, "Thank you," and a smile.

"Do you have any questions for me today?" I had to get down to business if Willa had any academic questions, but I didn't want to minimize my interest in her and Peggy.

"Oh! I have a question about a calculus assignment. Do you think you could help me with that? It's not geology."

"Lay it on me. I'll see if I can help, but it's been awhile since I took calculus."

It took me about ten seconds to remember the procedure for calculating a derivative by taking limits, but we worked together and found the proper result.

"Thanks for the math help. Now, I have a physics question." She turned to another page in her notebook. This went on for about ten minutes, but nothing about geology ever came up.

I laughed and said, "What's next, astronomy?"

Willa grinned, "No. You haven't gone far enough in the book to create enough material for a question about geology." She put her pencil down and looked at me. "Am I wasting your time?"

I smiled, "No, you could never waste my time. I must say I'm a little weak with English and the social sciences, if you can call them sciences. And I know very little biology."

"I know what you mean, I'm enrolled in beginning sociology, but I might drop it."

I had a question for Willa that had been brewing ever since I had seen her about four months ago. "I have a question that has been nagging at me for some time. Why were you a blonde when I saw you visiting with Dr. Reynolds?"

Willa smiled and looked at Peggy. "Peggy, do you remember when we came here a long time ago to see another man?"

She looked up from the crystal model parts, nodded, and said, "Uh-huh."

"Do you remember why momma's hair was yellow?"

Peggy nodded. "You had a wig—to hide the blue hair."

I couldn't help laughing. "You had blue hair?"

Willa was laughing, too. "I made a mistake. I wanted to put some blonde streaks in my hair, but I screwed up and it turned blue. I had to cover it up. It was terrible. I borrowed a neighbor's blonde wig."

"When you talked with Professor Reynolds, I saw you in the hallway, but I couldn't see what you looked like. When I saw Peggy at the crater with you and your husband, I realized you had been the woman I got a glimpse of in the hall. Why didn't you stop and say hello?"

"Steve was waiting for me in the car. I didn't have time to talk. I knew I would start to cry when we met and then Steve would wonder what was going on. I wanted to say hello and tell you I'd probably be in your class, but I couldn't."

"You never told him about me helping you learn to read?"

"Oh, no. He doesn't know that I had trouble learning to read. I know he'd tease me about being a slow learner. That would give him more ammunition for arguing against me going to college."

"Okay. I won't mention it to Gail then. We'll keep it between you and me."

Willa whispered to me and pointed at Peggy, "Don't say secret, she'll blab to Steve."

I gave her a thumbs up.

Willa stood up and said, "I've got to go. I have to register Peggy over at the children's center in the Education Building and then drive home."

"Where are you living?"

"It's a small housing project outside of Del Mar. Steve drives straight down Route 5 to the base. He's on a team that's updating destroyers. He's a welder."

"Gail told me that. She said her husband is a pipe fitter."

Willa nodded and reached down to help Peggy off the floor. "Come on, Peg, we have to go." She glanced at me and said, "Sorry about the mess, I'll help you pick up the pieces."

"No, you go ahead and take off. I'll get the stuff off the floor. It'll only take me a minute. Get Peggy registered and have a safe trip home. Will I see you tomorrow?"

"Yes. Bye—and thanks."

As I corralled the model pieces, I could hear Peggy's and Willa's footsteps growing fainter as they went down the hall toward the elevator. I placed the top back on the box of sticks and spheres and put the model kit in my desk drawer, ready for Peggy's next visit. I needed to get some toys she could play with while Willa and talk about her classes and anything else she cares to mention. As I sat there pondering, I wondered if I was ever going to get Willa out of my mind. If she is having marital difficulties, perhaps there's a chance for me despite the difference in our ages. I was curious if it would make any difference to her. I don't know when I would ask such a question, though, maybe never.

I got a cup of coffee and sat at my desk for a few minutes trying to avoid thinking about anything. I suddenly decided to visit the teaching lab to see if the assistant needed any help. I took the stairs and wasted about ten minutes; the TA didn't need any assistance. When I returned to my office, my coffee was cold, so I put it in the microwave for a minute on high. I had to get moving on my research idea so I continued with the list of phone numbers for museums. When I completed the table, I had seventy-three phone numbers in the US and forty-nine in foreign countries. I checked my office clock. Time to go home for dinner; it was five o'clock.

The short drive home was just long enough for me to realize I was going to exceed my phone budget for the entire year on this one project. I had to visit with the college dean and try to arrange for more funding. The long distance calls to foreign museums were going to eat up my yearly $1,000 allocation very quickly. I couldn't depend only on the stateside museums for the samples I needed, there might be some important ones overseas. While I ate dinner, I outlined my research plan in layman's terms so the dean would understand my proposal. Hopefully, I would be able to get an appointment to see Dean Cottrell on Friday, but she was almost always very busy, and Fridays were no exception.

I called the dean's office as soon as I arrived at my office Friday morning. It was 8:10. She wasn't in yet, but her secretary said I would get a call back when the dean was available.

My class was at ten o'clock, so I got some coffee and prepared some lecture notes. I was still going over tectonic plates and the formation of the continents in class, so I didn't need to spend much time preparing that topic. It seemed I had been over the features of the earth's crust many more times than had actually been the case, but I enjoyed talking about it.

At 9:45 the phone rang. It was the dean's secretary. She had scheduled me for a 2:00 p.m. meeting with Dr. Cottrell. I would have fifteen minutes to plead my case.

"Thanks for returning my call. I'll be there. Bye."

I was pretty sure the dean knew what isotopes were, but I jotted a few more notes so I would remember to avoid going over her head. Her doctorate was in English literature. I had no knowledge of how much science she knew. I made my explanation as simple as I could, justifying my argument for the funding increase. I had a premonition that she was going to refer me to the dean of research, whom I disliked. He had a gigantic ego, and in my opinion, bordered on megalomania. He enjoyed displaying his power, and in addition, his temper was easily triggered. I wasn't looking forward to another defensive one-sided conversation.

Maybe the dean would grant me some unused phone time from other professors. However, that might be improbable—some faculty members did most of their calling during the spring. Spring semester was the best time for recruiting for nearly all disciplines. Occasionally faculty recruitment extended through the summer and people were hired a week or two before fall semester started. That was my case. I had been hired two weeks before classes began. In that short period, I had been transformed from graduate student to assistant professor with four times the salary.

I was thinking about the meeting with the dean and the obstacles preventing my obtaining more funding as I walked to my ten o'clock, but when I arrived in the lecture hall, all my worries disappeared. Willa smiled when I entered the room and placed my class scribbles on the lectern. I felt a surge of confidence when Willa and I were in the same room. All it took was a glance and I couldn't help but return the smile. I was wondering if I was becoming obsessed with her, never having experienced those feelings before, but I had to keep my mind on my job. I'd have to focus on the faces on the other side of the room when I looked up from my notes.

At the end of my lecture, I was rushed by several students asking about the first exam. When would it be? Multiple choice or true-false? Were the questions of the essay type? When the group had dispersed, Willa and her buddy, Gail, were at the exit waiting for me to catch up with them.

The two women climbed the three steps to the hallway and they both said, "See you Monday," as they started the walk to exit the building.

Willa added, "Have a nice weekend."

I replied, "You, too." I secured my folder of notes in my right hand and began the trek to my office for lunch. After eating, I had to start preparing for my meeting with the dean.

On the way back to my office the Ten Commandments entered my thoughts. The one that was gnawing at me concerned coveting a neighbor's wife. But Willa's husband was not my neighbor; I didn't even know him and they lived in another town. I was conveniently ignoring the broader definition of neighbor.

But then it occurred to me that Willa might be brown nosing; using our previous friendship to gain some advantage when I graded her papers. I quickly dismissed that possibility. I couldn't believe Willa would do such a thing; she was just too honest. But then it had been sixteen years since I had worked with her—almost a generation, a nearly forgotten previous life. She had been an eight-year-old kid and I was an adult when I helped her learn to read. But, human beings change with time and life experiences, predominantly in a positive way, but occasionally in a negative manner.

CHAPTER 10

WHILE I killed time in my office waiting for my meeting with the dean, I decided to make a call to one of the museums on my list. I dialed the number in Arizona but the campus operator interrupted and told me I needed to dial nine to get an outside line. I had never made a long distance call from my office and had forgotten the procedure I had been given when I arrived on campus several years earlier.

The museum was in Phoenix, so I dialed a nine and then the ten-digit number and waited. After four rings a woman answered. I explained who I was and what I was looking for.

"I'll transfer you to Dr. Weems."

A woman answered, "I understand you want us to send you a meteorite."

"Not just an ordinary meteorite, doctor."

I repeated the same explanation as before, but with a more scientific terminology and added, "I don't need the entire meteorite. I just need a few milligrams of iron. I don't want a sample of a stony meteorite."

"All right. This will take some time. We have dozens of meteorites, some weighing several kilograms. I'll have to have one of our assistants make a list and get back to you in a few days. I'll transfer you to our answering service and they will get your number. I expect it might take a week before we reply. Please hold."

I held. After ten seconds, I was going to call this attempt a bust, but just as I was moving the phone away from my ear, a voice asked, "May I have your number, Dr. Curtis?"

I responded with my number and hung up. I leaned back in my chair. "Geez, this is going to take a lot of time and even more patience."

Frustration was creeping into my entire body. Acquiring the samples was going to be a major undertaking, and then I would have to run the mass spectra of the samples. I hadn't realized another problem I would encounter until I conferred with Dr. Grossman in the mass spec laboratory. My clock read 1:50. I had less than ten minutes to get to the dean's office after I reached ground level.

It took me over two minutes to get out of the Science Building, I should have taken the stairs; the elevator stopped three times before getting to street level. Someone said 'Hi' to me as I left the building. I didn't look to see who it was, but it probably was a colleague, most students in my classes had already left campus for the weekend.

I passed the Westcliff Library four minutes before my meeting, so I broke into a run. I couldn't be late and I had another 400 yards to go. I entered the big swinging glass doors and walked as fast as I could to the other end of the long hallway that terminated at the dean's office. I was out of breath when I sat down in the waiting area with one minute to spare.

The dean's door opened slowly and she appeared with a business-like expression. She was taller than I remembered, probably five-nine. She had on a white blouse, a Navy-blue skirt, and no shoes. She looked right at me and said, "Come in, Dr. Curtis."

My pulse had dropped to about 100. I stood and tried not to trip over my own feet. As I entered her office, the door closed behind me. I had never been in the dean's office and I was a bit nervous. I could smell a slight odor of some type of cleaning fluid, probably from the custodial service the previous evening. I looked around to see if there was any evidence of a pet.

She was a nice looking woman probably in her mid-forties. I wondered how she had become dean at such a young age. Most deans I had ever met were pushing sixty and looking forward to retirement. Her hair was nearly black and showed no vestiges of gray, but that could easily be explained by hair coloring.

"Have a seat." She pointed at a chair and I sat down as if it were an order from a military officer.

"Thank you." I almost said that I saw she had dressed for our meeting, but I kept my mouth closed. I didn't know if she had a sense of humor. I could hear the air conditioning fan in the ceiling.

"Pardon my bare feet. I was on my feet all morning and through lunch. I just got back here ten minutes ago and *had* to take off my shoes. I wore the uncomfortable ones today—bad choice." She smiled and picked up a pen from her desk. "Now, please tell me what you envision and how I can help."

That comment launched me into an explanation of my research, which took me about five minutes. Then she surprised me.

"So, you think you will be able to identify the source of a meteorite if you know the isotopes of the iron present?"

"Yes. When a meteorite is found and no one saw it fall, there is no way to tell the origin. If the isotopes from one radiant are nearly identical but differ from those of another radiant, it would give us a way of identifying the source—usually a comet, maybe from the Oort cloud."

"Yes, I can see the value in knowing that. What do you anticipate you'll need in funds?"

I told her there were over 120 museums on my list and about 40% were foreign based.

"All right. I have a contingency fund and I'll double your normal support for communications. If that isn't enough, let me know and I'll see if I can come up with more money. Is there anything else I can help you with?"

"No, Dr. Cottrell. Thank you very much. I was hoping I wouldn't have to see the research director. He is a difficult man."

She nodded, uttered, "I understand," and smiled.

I stood and she walked me to the exit. I opened the door and said, "Thanks again, Dean Cottrell."

"Thank you for being so brief. I enjoyed our talk."

As I walked down that long, cold, nearly vacant hallway, I figured I had at least one friend in high places. Thank God I didn't have to see the research dean. That would have ruined my day and my weekend.

During the weekend, I spent most of the daylight hours in my office and the library constructing a list of museums to contact that might offer the most useful samples. I ended up with forty-one numbers to call: seventeen foreign and the rest stateside, mostly on the East coast. I reasoned that most of the population centers were in the east, so more meteorites found would be from known radiants. I would find out if my assumptions were correct as I began placing calls and determining my success rate. I knew it was going to be a slow process. Much of my success depended on the museums and the curators' desire to assist me in the study.

I was a bit surprised, but pleased, when I arrived on campus Monday. The first thing I usually did when arriving in the science building was to swing by the department office. My usually empty mailbox contained a FAX from the Phoenix museum. It gave me a list of phone numbers and names of curators and technicians of all museums in the Southwestern United States that contained meteorites.

I was to contact Dr. Gary Beatty for assistance at the Phoenix location. Things were looking up! When I reached my office, I found a note taped to my door. Dr. Reynolds wanted to see me. I put my book and notes on my desk and walked down the hall to Ethan's office. The door was open and he was on the phone. He motioned for me to enter and take a seat. I had no idea what he wanted to see me about.

Apparently he was talking to his wife because he said, "Bye, dear," and hung up. He was too straight-laced to have a mistress. He turned to me and said, "I heard you talked to the dean." The tone of his voice and facial expression made it an accusation, not a statement of fact.

"Yes, sir. I asked her for a supplement to my phone allotment and she granted me an extra $1,000."

"But you went over my head. Why?" He snapped angrily.

"I didn't think much about it. When we had our department meeting the other day, you complained about the tight budget, so I assumed you had no other resources. Was I wrong?"

He glared at me with those beady eyes and answered, "Well, no. But you should have asked me first. You know there is a chain of command."

I thought for a moment. I was going to say something about it not being a military operation, but I kept it to myself.

"I felt sure what you would say, so I went where there was a chance for success. I could have seen the research dean, also, but I don't get along very well with him, so I pursued the next best option."

"Well, if there is a next time, I'd like you to consult with me before you go to the dean. Is that understood?"

"Yes, sir. Is that all?"

He nodded and looked away. "You are dismissed." I went back to my office feeling like I had just visited the grade school principal's office for pulling a girl's pigtails and was paddled. What a waste of time and words. That little meeting did not strengthen my opinion of Reynolds. Next time, if the bathroom needs a roll of toilet paper, I'll check with the chairman first—before I talk with the custodian. I doubt that will ever happen, but just for insurance purposes, I'll keep an extra roll in my office. Then I'll be accused of hoarding ass wipe.

After my blood pressure and pulse assumed normal values, I placed five long distance calls to museums in the Carolinas and Georgia. Four of the five contacts were positive. Each museum had from three to five samples to send me. The specimens would arrive the following week. I was reminded to acknowledge the museums in my publication. I began to wonder if my voice didn't sound intellectual enough. The museum people must think I don't know how to write a research paper.

Early Sunday morning, about 1:30 a.m., a bright light illuminated the sky in Southern California. The 911 calls were questions about a rocket launch, a plane crash and alien invaders. I was asleep at the time and didn't find out about it until I turned on the TV at 7:00 a.m. I wondered if any meteorites would be discovered.

Not long after eating lunch, I received a call at home from one of the astronomers at Ocean Vista. Dr. Mitch Allen wanted to know if I would like to accompany him and two graduate students to Death Valley where a small impact crater had formed. The bright light from the bolide had been reported from Mexico to Oregon and in Arizona and Nevada. Dr. Allen said the radiant was known, so that piqued my interest.

I had run into Mitch at McDonald's Friday evening and we had talked about our research interests. By chance we saw each other at the restaurant. He was buying his ten-year-old son an ice cream cone after attending a high school football game. I was getting some coffee and a burger on my way home after working past my normal dinner time.

When he heard of the bolide, he felt sure I would be interested in recovering a piece of meteorite for my study.

CHAPTER 11

ITCH WAS right. I immediately called Dr. Reynolds to inform him of my plans to go to Death Valley for two days with Dr. Allen. He said it was fine with him as long as my classes were covered. I got on the phone to my TA, Miss McCain, to ask her to take my lectures on Monday and Tuesday. She was flattered that I had that much confidence in her teaching. I told her I would leave lecture outlines in my departmental mailbox.

I dialed Mitch's number and said, "It's a go with me, Mitch. I've got my classes covered and permission from my department chair."

"Great! I'll pick you up in the morning at 6:00 a.m."

"Sounds good. I'll be waiting."

I sat by the phone for a few minutes trying to bring to mind everything I had to do before six o'clock in the morning. My lecture classes were most important, so I drove over to the Science Building and took the elevator to the sixth floor. I made sure I had the correct notes for Monday/Tuesday classes, both texts, and put everything in a small box with a note attached. I addressed the note to Beth asking her to give the box to Marsha McCain Monday morning. I placed the box on Beth's chair where it would be impossible for her to miss it. I then scribbled a note for Marsha and stuck it in her graduate student mailbox. I locked the office and returned home. The maneuver to the two offices had taken only thirty minutes.

Back home, I checked on the weather for Death Valley during September and gathered appropriate clothing. The high temperatures would be close to 100 degrees and the lows about 70. I wouldn't need much clothing for two days, but I packed a long-sleeve shirt, two sets of underwear, and three pairs of socks. I thought one pair of pants would be enough. I had a straw hat from desert expeditions and a couple of canteens.

I filled the canteens with water and placed them in the refrigerator to cool overnight. I crammed all my things in a knapsack a little larger than a small overnight bag. The canteens would hang from my belt.

I sat at the kitchen table and made a list of must-have items, besides clothing, for the outing. I listed absolute everything I could think of and took a shower to give me a rest and clear my mind. When in the shower, I realized I had forgotten my diabetic supplies; I felt really stupid. The excitement of going on the search for meteorites had dulled my most important senses.

I wasn't sure who was going on the trip, so I tossed in a stick of deodorant. I didn't think any women would be going, but I didn't want to gross them out smelling like men's locker-room dirty socks and jockstraps.

The last item on my list was the metal detector. It was in the trunk of my car. The batteries were new, so I didn't have to worry about charging or replacing them. Just in case, I taped an extra set to the handle of the detector.

I hardly slept that night and was up and sipping hot coffee at 5:00 a.m. I went through my list one last time, couldn't think of anything else, set everything next to the door, and fixed breakfast. I was ready to go at 5:40 and I turned on the TV to hear if there was any news about the streak of light that lit up Southern California early Sunday morning.

There was a brief recap saying astronomers from Mt. Palomar Observatory and representatives from the Air Force were investigating. It had been confirmed a satellite re-entering the atmosphere was not responsible for the bright light.

A couple of minutes before six o'clock a knock at my apartment door caused me to turn off the television and go to the door. I expected to see Mitch, but it was a young woman, not much over five feet tall and very pretty. Though the morning sunlight was not yet bright, my porchlight caused her eyes to sparkle. She wore a loose fitting white shirt tucked into jeans with no belt. I couldn't help noticing her nice figure. I also saw that she was wearing a wedding ring, but it wasn't ostentatious; at best it was a quarter carat diamond or maybe cubic zirconia.

My immediate thought was she must be Mitch's daughter. She appeared to be a teenager, but that was before I saw the ring and heard her speak.

"I'm Lisa Landers, a graduate student of Dr. Allen's. Can I help you carry anything?"

I extended my hand and said, "It's nice to meet you. I didn't know Mitch had any female students." When we shook hands, I noticed her grip was very delicate, but firm. It crossed my mind that she might be a musician, perhaps a violinist, besides being a stargazer.

She laughed, almost a giggle, and replied, "I'm not considered a female in astronomy, just a slave laborer."

She stepped through the doorway, picked up my metal detector, one of my canteens, and started down the stairs. I followed with my bag and the other canteen. Mitch climbed out of the station wagon, opened the rear door, and Lisa slid the detector in the back. Mitch tossed my bag in with the other luggage. I assumed the male sitting in the front passenger seat was a graduate student.

Lisa got in behind Mitch and I slid in behind the student riding copilot. I studied the back of his head and decided he looked older than a typical graduate student. He was about my size, wore glasses and a five o'clock shadow.

Mitch said, "Ned, I'd like you to meet Dr. Dick Nielsen. He's from the Palomar Observatory. Dick, this is Dr. Ned Curtis, a geologist at Ocean Vista."

Dick turned about ninety degrees and we shook hands awkwardly over the front seat. We both smiled and nodded. I was sure Mitch would fill me in on the background of Lisa and Dr. Nielsen. I felt like I was going off to summer camp.

Mitch was a typical California driver and we shot forward into the street, made a right turn, almost on two wheels, and headed toward the mountains at ten miles per hour over the limit. I was going to ask where we were going when Mitch spoke up, "It'll take us about ten minutes to get to the McClellan-Palomar Airfield. We're taking the university plane to the Amargosa Airport on route 127."

"Who's the university pilot?" I didn't know the university had a pilot.

Mitch looked at Dick and grinned. "I am for today. Dick flies too."

Jokingly, I said, "Ah, I'd better not go today. Take me back home, please."

Dick reacted. "You're not serious, are you?"

"No." I laughed and Lisa said, "That was a good one." She smiled at me and I interpreted it as a touch of admiration.

I always liked to get off to a good start when meeting new people. I found that humor had always stimulated a relaxed conversation and participants were not exhibiting much, if any, artificiality. Of course, I had run into a few straight-laced individuals that didn't seem to care for my humor; Dr. Reynolds was one of those persons. I felt sorry they were bound to such strict behavior.

When we were in the air, I leaned forward on my seat to watch the altimeter as we rose above most of the Southern California Mountains. Mitch leveled the plane at 8,000 feet. Our flight time seemed very short. Lisa and I watched the terrain as we talked about our academic backgrounds for the majority of the eighty-five minute flight. I was impressed with her intellectual level and maturity. Her marriage never entered the conversation, except that her husband, Brian, worked for a computer company in San Francisco. I didn't think it was any of my business to ask her why she wasn't in Northern California or why her husband hadn't found employment in the LA area.

Mitch rented a large SUV in Death Valley Junction for our drive to the impact site. It took us an hour to get to Badwater and another forty minutes to reach the small crater. We were stopped by the State Patrol once and twice by the military. Once we showed them our identification, they let us pass, giving us directions to the site. The military check point nearest the crater had us exit the vehicle for a search. When they realized we were legit, they were very cordial and asked if we needed any water or gas.

We convinced the authorities we were self-sufficient. Mitch drove another mile along a temporary dirt road recently graded to enable easy access to the crater which was on the side of a hill with a twenty degree slope. There were three vehicles at the site: two pickups with attached campers, and a medium size RV from Mt. Wilson Observatory. A grader had cleared a two tiered parking space for about half-a-dozen small vehicles.

Mitch and Dick knew one of the investigators from Mt. Wilson. They shook hands and began an animated conversation, pointing at the crater, then toward the sky. Lisa and I watched and waited in our car as the three investigators seemed to be joking. I began to wonder how serious the men were about the examination of the crater.

We could see the asymmetric rim of the crater, similar to the mountainous ring of earth surrounding the Winslow meteor crater, but in miniature. The raised earth was about four to five feet above the surrounding terrain on the downside of a hill, and only two feet on the uphill portion of the crater. Lisa and I got out of the SUV and took a closer look at the depression. It looked to me to be about thirty feet long and twenty feet wide so was elliptical.

"Go ahead and scan the outside of the crater with your metal detector, Ned. Some fragments have already been picked up." Mitch was speaking from about thirty feet away where he was talking to other researchers. Lisa heard Mitch and pulled my detector from the SUV and brought it over to me. She also had a small notebook and pen for recording the coordinates of anything we found. I was impressed with her intuition. She seemed to anticipate where I was going to search with the instrument when I climbed to the uphill edge of the rim.

Lisa had drawn an ellipse showing the outward stake reference points marked with compass directions. She and I spent about forty-five minutes scanning the area around the crater and found some small iron fragments less than an inch in size, which we placed in plastic bags marked with labels as to their locations. When we completed our scan, we had collected seventeen small fragments, some as small as peas.

Mitch came over to us and said, "The crew from Mt. Wilson will complete a thermal scan of the interior in a few minutes, then you can search for iron debris inside the crater."

I nodded and sat down in the SUV with Lisa. The sun was starting to heat up the area, but we didn't expect the temperature to rise much above eighty degrees because of our altitude at 4,100 feet. The thermal reading on the valley floor was expected to top out near the century mark.

"What kind of music do you like?" Lisa asked. She scooted a bit closer to me and glanced up with those glittering eyes. She had undone two buttons at the top of her shirt. She was really hot—not from the temperature. I couldn't help noticing her cleavage. I glanced away to look out the window. I didn't want my interest to be too obvious.

I had to redirect my thoughts in a split second. "Ah, piano, classical, and easy listening. I like Wagner and the Narada collections. How about you?"

Her left hand briefly touched my thigh when she leaned back into the cushioned seat. My question seemed to have gotten her interest away from whatever she had been planning.

"I love classical music—actually orchestral of all types. I play the oboe, the piano, and the harp. I really love the harp."

In the school band, I had played the trombone, but not very well. I didn't bother to bring it up; it was not one of my accomplishments.

"When you came to my door this morning, I thought your hands were those of a musician. You have a very delicate touch."

"Oh, thank you." She scooted another inch closer.

I felt like running my hand up her thigh, but only for a second. My better judgement stopped me from doing something stupid. I had no idea what would happen, but I imagined the worst. What if she were unconscious of what I considered provocative actions? I found that thought to be almost unbelievable, but I couldn't risk following my temptations. The little sex devil on my right shoulder was being overruled by the angelic one on my left.

Mitch appeared at the open back door of the SUV, leaned in and grabbed a camera from his belongings. As he checked the camera, he said, "Ned, you can search the inside of the crater now. The thermal imaging team has completed their scan. Lisa, you can help me with the pictures. I'll need you to hold a meter stick for scale."

Lisa slid out the passenger side of the vehicle. As I picked up the metal detector she passed by and said, "I'd like to talk with you some more if you don't mind."

"Sure—on our way back in the plane. I'd enjoy that."

She smiled at me, took the meter stick from Mitch and followed him and Dr. Nielsen as they photographed the crater rim and bottom.

I found eleven more meteorites inside the crater, mostly fragments about the size of small marbles. Some of the fragments were six to eight inches beneath the surface and were exposed by digging with a small trowel. Anything deeper couldn't be detected with my equipment, but I thought the thermal scan might show something.

Lisa was standing above me at the rim. "Dr. Curtis, Dr. Allen said we're going to have some lunch in the SUV. Have you finished here?"

"Yes. I'll be there in just a minute. Thanks for summoning me, my stomach is growling."

While we ate lunch, we listened to music and talk-radio. Callers to the talk show kept coming back to alien invasion when the illumination from the bolide came up. Mitch turned off the radio when stupidity reached his boiling point. We all agreed with his reaction. As we were finishing our drinks and sandwiches, Dr. Arnold Keitmer from Mt. Wilson approached the vehicle.

"Mitch, take a look at the thermal imaging scan. It looks like there's a hot spot several feet below the surface. I've ordered a backhoe to dig it up, but it'll be another hour before the equipment arrives."

Keitmer showed the computer printout to Mitch and Dick. Mitch handed the data back to me to review the results. I turned the sheet of paper to Lisa, but she was sliding over next to me and I dropped the data sheet to the floor.

"Sorry. Let me get it. I reached down and felt her hand on my back, a subtle touching."

I raised back up and together we held the paper so we could both observe the location of the warm mass beneath the bottom of the depression. I noticed she was watching my eyes. She glanced at the thermal map and commented, "The mass is off center so we can calculate the approximate angle when it hit."

I had already guessed that it might have come from Perseus, but it was not a normal Perseid meteor, arriving too late in the year to be part of the normal Perseid shower of August. Lisa had the same opinion that I did so we thought it was just a chunk of an asteroid that happened to come near the earth—not an unusual occurrence.

We had a short discussion with Mitch. He was of the opinion we should head back home but Dick wanted to stay and see the backhoe unearth the buried portion of the meteorite. I thought I would like to see what was dug up and so did Lisa. Mitch was outvoted, so he went to work trying to calculate the path of the bolide. In the meantime, Dick, Lisa, and I hiked to the top of the hill and scanned the terrain to the horizon. I anticipated Lisa getting tired of climbing and wanting to rest, but she was a real trooper, staying with Dick and me to the crest.

We could see the backhoe coming up the mountain on a truck, but when about a quarter of a mile away from the crater, it was unloaded and chugged up the hill to do the digging, leaving the flatbed behind.

CHAPTER 12

THE BACKHOE driver left the engine idling, dropped to the ground, adjusted his pants, and talked with Dr. Keitmer. The men shook hands and the driver climbed back in the operator's seat and began digging a trench through the crater rim on the downhill portion of raised earth. We all watched as the trench got deeper and deeper until it was ten feet below the bottom of the cavity. Dr. Keitmer put his fingers to his lips and whistled to get the attention of the backhoe operator. Keitmer signaled with a hand across his throat and the driver cut the engine. The sudden quiet was so abrupt I could almost hear my heart beating, but that was not unusual for the solitude I had experienced on the desert floor on other excursions. I could hear air passing through my nostrils with every breath.

The operator walked over to Professor Keitmer and said, "Doctor, there's nothing there, just soil. You want me to go deeper?"

"No. You can go now. We're finished here. Thanks for coming out to help us."

"You bet. Where do I send the paperwork?"

"Mt. Wilson Observatory. Your boss knows the address. Thanks again."

The backhoe engine came to life and the driver started back toward the flatbed. We gathered around Dr. Keitmer.

Mitch asked, "What was your conclusion, doctor?"

"The earth was compacted and heated. At that depth it took a while to cool, that's all. We're only going to get fragments; the object exploded on impact. I'm ready to go—there is nothing to keep us here to investigate. I'll send a notice to the media."

The group dispersed and individuals headed to their various vehicles. We were the second party to leave the scene. As we descended the hill, the temperature began to climb, but we were comfortable in the air-conditioned SUV. Lisa was quiet on the way back to the airport and I didn't have much to say, either. I was thinking about the analysis of the fragments we had accumulated and I broke the silence just before we arrived at our plane.

"Thank you for helping me gather the samples, Lisa. I rarely have anyone to help; I am usually out in the field alone. I'm thinking about getting a pooch."

She hit me with another enticing-eyes smile and replied, "You're welcome. It was fun to help. Geology studies are way different than collecting astronomical data. Astronomers rarely contact the objects they are investigating; stars are light years away—except for the sun. Let me know if I can help you again. I'll give you my number and address if you want to get in touch."

On the return flight to McClellan-Palomar airport, Lisa fell asleep leaning against the cabin wall. I wanted to wake her when I noticed her cheek was getting deformed against the plastic cockpit wall, but I was afraid she would tip towards me and put her head on my shoulder or my lap. I didn't want Mitch and Dick to get the wrong idea, but I wouldn't have minded donating my shoulder to the pretty young lady for half an hour.

She woke up as we started descending from altitude and asked me, "Did I miss anything?"

"Yeah. We told a bunch of dirty jokes after you fell asleep."

She surprised me when she said, "I've probably heard them all before. I don't think I missed anything after all." She started laughing and I couldn't take my eyes off her. I was laughing, too. Then she said, "What? You're staring at me."

"I can't help it. Your eyes sparkle when you smile or laugh. But I'm sure you know that."

I think I embarrassed her a little; she continued smiling but didn't say anything more until they dropped me off at my apartment. She carried my metal detector up to my door, pulled a slip of paper from her pocket, and said, "Here's my number and address. Drop in sometime and I'll show you around the observatory." She handed me the paper torn from her notepad. I folded it and stuck it in my shirt pocket.

"I'll do that, provided I can get away from campus. I've got to get a paper published before spring semester is over. I'm not going to have much free time."

"Maybe I'll come see you. I promise not to get in your way. Bye."

I watched her sexy figure go down the stairs and walk to the SUV. As she got in the car, she rose on her tiptoes to see me over the car door and waved. I waved back and watched the SUV go to the corner, make a right turn, and vanish behind the homes next to the other quadruplex. I unlocked the door and entered with my bag and detector, sat on the sofa, and closed my eyes. All I could see was Lisa's eyes. In a way, though, I was glad she was gone. I had two other important matters to think of: Willa and my research, but Lisa had generated some overwhelming temptations. I had to get Lisa out of my mind. I had no choice.

The immediate task was to call Marsha and let her know I was back. She wouldn't have to lecture on Tuesday. That would take a load off her mind. She would be able to devote her time to prepping the lab if that hadn't already been done. I remembered I had given her my text, but I had my lecture notes filed in my office cabinet. I'd break them out of storage in the morning when I arrived at my desk.

Tuesday morning passed quickly. I was able to get all the meteorite samples cataloged and after I checked my mailbox, I went over to see Dr. Grossman in the mass spectroscopy laboratory. When I asked if he or his graduate students could run my samples, I found it was not going to be an easy task. The samples were going to have to be complexed with an organic agent in order to get the iron analyzed.

The melting point of the iron in the meteorites is extremely high, and the boiling point even higher. It would be difficult to get any metallic iron in the gas phase to complete an isotopic analysis. I hadn't expected to be doing any chemistry, but the reactions were not complicated. Dr. Grossman informed me the complex of iron I wanted was bright red.

I stopped by Dr. Gupta's office in the chemistry section of the building and he gave me a reagent bottle of acetyl acetone to react with the metallic iron samples to produce the red crystalline product I needed. When I returned to my office, I placed several more calls to museums on the East Coast. At eleven o'clock I had lunch, locked my office, and made more calls during the noon hour time period. I opened my door at 1:00 p.m. and anticipated Willa showing up, but no one arrived during my office hours. I was disappointed that no students had dropped in to see me, but it was still very early in the semester; questions would arise later on. I especially missed seeing and talking with Willa.

After thirty minutes of waiting for students, I went to my adjoining laboratory and prepared a small sample of the tris-acetylacetonate iron crystals. I recrystallized the red material and let it air dry. I was going to submit the sample to the mass spectroscopy lab in the morning. I shut down my lab at 4:30, went in my office, and made a couple of calls to museums in the Northeastern US. Two more samples were going to be sent to me for analysis.

Just as I was about to leave for dinner there was a knock on my door. It was Marsha returning my textbooks. We talked a few minutes about my trip to the crater and walked to the elevator together. I got off the elevator on the third floor, checked my mailbox in the office, and found a small package from Tucson. I took it home with me; there was no sense in returning to my office. I'd open it in the morning and clean out a couple of lab bench drawers for samples that were going to arrive in the next few weeks. I had to be meticulous about labeling and recording data with regard to the various meteorite specimens. If I screwed up one sample, it could create a relatively large dispersion in the data. I was hoping for very small standard deviations. But the solar system has a mind of its own; I'm wondering if my original idea was just a shot in the dark.

The remainder of the week passed by quickly. No students came by with questions and I began to wonder if Willa had lost interest in our periods of visiting. But she had her family to contend with and I decided to spend my time totally involved with my research activities. Willa and Gail sat together in lecture but I didn't receive the slightest acknowledgement from either of them, no waves or smiles were displayed during class or as they left after the lectures. I was disappointed, but what could I do? I was in no position to meddle in their relationships. Besides, they were acting like normal students, listening to my words of wisdom, taking notes, and going to their next class, studying, or doing any number of other things students do.

As I worked on my research, cataloging, sorting and labeling meteoric material, I occasionally slipped into thinking about Willa and Peggy, but those thoughts twisting in my mind became more fleeting as the weekend passed. Seventeen samples for analysis required being on the ball preventing stupid mistakes. I didn't even turn on the radio during my laboratory work, but as I progressed, I started humming. At one time I had to laugh, I was humming a Christmas carol: "Silent Night." It could have been "Silent Lab."

I had to process one sample at a time to eliminate any possible mix-up. I weighed a small amount of the first sample, dissolved it in acid and then neutralized the solution with base. I filtered off the iron hydroxide and added it to a small amount of acetyl acetone, added a little ethyl alcohol and stirred. Almost immediately, the solution began turning red, and as the red color became darker and darker, I couldn't help becoming excited. I recorded my procedure and color changes in my notebook. The lab became quiet; my humming had turned to smiles.

As I warmed the red solution to remove the alcohol, red crystals began to form, so I set the little Erlenmeyer flask aside and watched the crystals grow and precipitate. When the alcohol and the slight excess of acetyl acetone had been evaporated, I put the crystals in a sample bottle and attached a label.

I noted the time and over an hour had passed processing that first sample. I was probably going to have hundreds more before coming to any conclusions. I wasn't going to have much, if any, spare time until all the samples were processed, which would require most of the work to be done on the weekends when I wouldn't be interrupted. The processing also involved obtaining the mass spectrum of each specimen. Research like this was not for the faint-hearted. This project was going to be a war: Curtis vs. iron.

The specimen I had chosen for the first analysis was a tiny piece of the bolide from the Death Valley excursion. I would remember that sample because I had collected it myself and it was the initial specimen processed chemically. I was able to process five samples on Saturday, another five on Sunday, and I hoped I could get another seven done during the following week. I still had nearly three dozen museums to contact, but I thought I could squeeze in some calls when I had a few minutes between other duties. If no one showed up for my office hours, I could get two more fragments processed, one Tuesday and one Thursday right after lunch. If the number of samples grew to what I had originally imagined, I hoped to get the study completed by Christmas.

Sunday evening was my time for lecture preparation for the coming week. As I was reviewing the text for my ten o'clock, I suddenly thought if I had some help, I could process the iron samples much faster. I'd have to ask Beth if any work-study students would qualify to work in my lab. I didn't have much hope of a positive response since most work-study students were business majors, not science majors. I needed a student with a background in chemistry. I'd mention it to Beth in the morning.

I arrived at the department office at 8:00 a.m., almost simultaneously with Beth. I was about ten feet from the door when she was turning the key in the lock. She hadn't noticed me, so I read some bulletin board material before entering the office. I wanted to give her a chance to get organized before I started asking questions. I heard her chair move and squeak so I went in to say the usual.

"Good morning. How's everything?"

She had just turned on her electric typewriter and I startled her. Beth was about my age but had three kids. Her husband was a vegetable farmer. She was a bit overweight, had short, graying hair and wore wire-rim glasses.

"Oh!" She dropped the paper she was trying to feed into her typewriter. She smiled, "Hi, Dr. Curtis. Good morning. How can I help you?"

I explained my idea about finding a work-study student with a chemistry background, and she said she would ask the financial aids people. Offhand, she couldn't think of anyone that fit the bill. I thanked her and checked my mailbox. There was a letter and a small package waiting for me. I assumed the package was from a museum, so I stuck it under my arm and using my finger, opened the envelope. It was a letter from a biography company. They wanted to include my name in a book about up-and-coming PhD's. I could have my mini bio included for the trifling amount of sixty dollars. I tore the letter in half, dropped it in the trash, and headed for my office.

As usual, I took the stairs to the sixth floor. On the way up, I examined the little package that was left in my mailbox. It wasn't from a museum; it was from Lisa Landers. I sat down at my desk and tore off the tan wrapping paper, saving the return address. I was wondering if it was the same as the address she had given me with her phone number. I couldn't compare the addresses, the sheet of paper she had given me was still in my shirt pocket in my bedroom closet. I had forgotten about it and probably would have washed my shirt without checking for the address.

It was a plastic cassette case. I flipped it over and there was a note attached to it. "Hope you enjoy the tape. I made it especially for you—Lisa." The only tape player I had was in my Pontiac. I would discover what was on the tape when I ate lunch in my car and listened to the recording. My curiosity was set on high, but I wasn't going to let my imagination run amuck. I wondered if she was serious about us getting together.

It was 8:30; ninety minutes until my ten o'clock class, so I went in the lab and processed another meteorite sample. I finished the crystallization, stored the crystals in a small sample vial, and attached a label. The next twenty minutes were spent going over my lecture notes and checking a few facts in the text. Then I was off to lecture.

CHAPTER 13

I WAS PLEASANTLY surprised when I arrived in class. Gail, Willa, and little Peggy were sitting together, the women talking. When I saw them, Willa smiled and waved, said something to Peggy and she waved both hands enthusiastically. I wasn't sure she remembered coming to my office two weeks earlier. Maybe Willa just told her to wave both hands. I was a little concerned that Peggy might not make it through a fifty minute lecture without squirming, but I was confident Willa could handle any problems that might arise. I noticed the little one was sitting on a folded blanket.

Willa had prepared for Peggy getting bored with the lecture and had supplied the youngster with a coloring book and Crayons. There was plenty of room for a little girl to lie on the floor either in front of or behind her mom if she needed to nap. It occurred to me a small child might fall asleep and wake up screaming, not recognizing where she was. That would undoubtedly add some excitement to the lecture. The auditorium style classroom might be an intimidating place for a child of three.

But the scenario I had imagined didn't take place. Peggy scribbled in a notebook while I lectured. As the students exited after lecture, Willa and Peggy stopped for a few seconds before leaving the big room. I had a sudden thought and asked if I could buy them lunch, but Willa declined. Peggy pulled at Willa's dress and said something I didn't catch.

"I have to take Peg to the Children's Center and meet Gail for lunch but thank you. Maybe some other time?"

"Sure, another time."

As Willa led Peggy out the door, she turned toward me, smiled, and said, "I'll see you tomorrow."

The smile she gave me seemed to indicate everything was all right. I reflected back to the week before when both she and Gail had been expressionless in class. What was going on? I hoped I'd find out in about twenty-six hours.

I heard my office phone ringing as I walked from the elevator, but I was too late to answer. Beth would take a message for me if the call were important. I'd find out after lunch. I grabbed my sandwich and apple and the tape from Lisa and headed for my car. When I got in the driver's seat of my Pontiac, I nearly burned my butt on the hot vinyl seat. After opening all the doors and lowering the windows, I got back in the car, this time in the back seat; it had been in the shade of the roof and was much cooler. Now I didn't have access to my tape player—what an idiot.

I remained in the back seat until my sandwich and apple had been consumed. I was thirsty and had to pee, so I got in the driver's seat, started the engine, put the tape in the dash player and drove home listening to the music Lisa had provided. I couldn't decide what the first song meant if anything. It was *I'd Like to Get to Know You* by Spanky and Our Gang. The rest of the tracks were piano-and-orchestra tunes by Roger Williams and Henri Mancini. I only had time to listen to three tracks of the tape while I drove home and back to campus. I'd listen to the remainder of the tape as I drove home in the evening and back to campus in the morning.

While home, I remembered to get Lisa's address from my shirt pocket. I wanted to check the address she had given me at Death Valley with the one on the package. If they were the same, she must not be living with another person other than her husband who was in San Francisco. I supposed that she could have a roommate, though. I was a little suspicious, to say the least. She sure seemed to be coming on to me and after meeting for only a few hours. What was she planning? I kind of hoped she was sincere, but I was a one woman at a time man. What was going to happen with Willa and Peggy?

Willa appeared at my office door promptly at 1:00 p.m. Tuesday.

"Hi! Come on in. How have you been?"

She came in and sat down on the edge of the chair in front of my desk and leaned forward toward the front of my desk.

"I want to apologize for ignoring you last week. Gail and I were having a rough time. She thinks I'm acting too emotionally. I value her friendship, so I tried not to say or do anything that would upset her."

I frowned and didn't say anything. I really didn't know where she was going with her statements. I thought I'd better just sit and listen.

She turned and looked at the open door. "Do you mind if I close the door?"

"No. It's all right with me, but don't lock it. Someone might misinterpret a locked office door. I don't want rumors to start floating across campus that I'm fooling around with pretty coeds in my office."

She laughed, shut the door, then returned to her chair, sat back down and said, "Gail thinks I should pray for guidance with my marriage problems, but she wants to keep a low profile and not be argumentative. But I have a difficult time with that advice. I'm not particularly religious."

I had no clue what to say, but I was wondering if I had anything to do with her problems. I had an idea. I wondered if Willa would talk differently if we were not in my office.

"Would you like to get some coffee off campus? We could go to a McDonald's or some other place for coffee."

"I'd like that, but someone might see us and it would get back to my husband. I don't know what would happen then. He has a temper and is super critical."

"Has he ever hit you?"

Willa shook her head.

"Well, if he ever did, it would be the last time he ever struck you. I can't stand it when a man hits a woman, and it would really piss me off if he hit you."

Willa didn't say anything, but I was thinking she probably thought I wasn't very strong. But I had been in wrestling matches with friends, sometimes larger than me, and I held my own. However, I'd never been in a fist fight before. I had to smile, thinking of having to take off my glasses before the first punch was thrown.

Willa frowned, "You just smiled. You're not serious?"

"Oh, I'm serious. I was thinking about finding someone to hold my glasses."

Willa laughed and said, "I'd hold them for you."

We both laughed.

"Tell me about your trip to Death Valley. Miss McCain said you would be gone for two days. You only missed Monday's classes."

I related the entire trip to Willa, mentioning Lisa's actions. When I finished my narrative, Willa said, "I think she really likes you."

"Could be, but she's married. Her husband is in San Francisco."

"That would be convenient." Willa grinned and raised her eyebrows. "I was going to ask you if you have a girlfriend. I guess it's none of my business." She looked down at her notebook.

I shook my head. "No. No girlfriend. I've been so busy for the last fifteen years, and almost always broke, I've never gotten involved with anyone. I've never gone out much—ever. I don't drink and I have to watch my diet, take medication at the same time every day, and get rest. I've been a loner since I was a teenager and never have appreciated social things. They made me too uncomfortable."

Willa leaned back and smiled, apparently watching my expression. I was wondering if she thought I was being truthful. I was.

"My husband will be leaving for work on the East Coast after Christmas. He wants me to go with him, but I'm going to stay here and take more classes. I don't want to take courses at a bunch of different universities and lose continuity. Some credits might not even transfer. I'm halfway to graduation now and I don't have a major, but I love geology. I'm sure with a degree in geology I'll be able to find a good job after graduation."

I was in support of her decision. "I think you're right about that. Women are under-represented in the sciences. Geology, chemistry, physics, astronomy, and biology could all use more women scientists, but unfortunately girls haven't had much encouragement to delve into disciplines that have been male dominated for so long. Most elementary school teachers are women and they don't seem to encourage girls to investigate the sciences because they didn't."

We sat in silence for a few seconds. Willa stood up and said, "I've got to go. I have to pick up Peggy early today. I'm taking her to a playmate's birthday party. I've been wondering if you would like to come over for dinner sometime."

I didn't answer immediately. I stood up and moved toward the door. "I'd like to come over and meet your husband. Also, I want you to tell me more about your years in elementary and high school." I opened the door and glanced down the hall, expecting to see someone caught listening. Willa stood next to me, looking up and smiling.

"Oh, I don't mean soon. I was thinking you could come over after my husband has gone to the East Coast. Peggy and I both like you. Peggy likes to help make stew and spaghetti—she loves spaghetti."

Her smile was intoxicating; I knew I shouldn't accept, but I couldn't refuse the invitation. "Sounds good, Willa."

"Remember, Dr. Curtis, it's not a date." She smiled again and winked.

"Have a good trip home with Peggy. Careful on the highway."

I watched her walk down the hall toward the elevator. I knew I wasn't going to be able to get her out of my mind any time soon, maybe never. When she disappeared around the corner, I could hear the faint sounds of the elevator doors open and close. I stood in my doorway gazing down the long hallway for several minutes, staring but seeing nothing. Then I went to my lab and started work on another sample. I had to get Willa out of my mind. My research required undivided attention.

When watching red crystals precipitate out of solution after I placed the Erlenmeyer flask in a small, ice bath. I was startled by the phone ringing.

"Hello?"

"Hi, Dr. Curtis. Did you get the package I sent?"

I thought it was one of the many museum curators asking about a meteorite specimen, so I said, "Which sample are you referring to?"

I heard some gentle laughter. "The music sample, Doctor."

"Oh! It's you, Lisa. I'm sorry. I didn't recognize your voice. I thought the call was about my research."

"No." She tittered, "It's about my research. I wanted to tell you I'm going to be taking a course in advanced thermodynamics in your building next semester. Dr. Gena Addario is scheduled to teach a graduate class and it will be taught Wednesday and Friday evenings. Do you mind if I come see you for some help once in a while?"

"Will you be on campus during the day, or just in the evenings?"

"Well, the lectures are from 6:30 to 8:00. I'd be out of class after 8:00 p.m. Would you be in your office then?"

"I can be. In fact, I'll probably be here most nights. I'm synthesizing metal complexes so I can get isotope distributions of the iron in meteorites. I think I told you about my work when we were on the plane. Oh! Thanks for the tape. You recorded just what I like."

"You're welcome. How about the first track?"

"I thought that was very clever. You know, that works both ways."

"Oops. I just looked at the time. I'd better let you go. I'll see you next semester."

I laughed, "Is that a promise or a threat?"

"That's a promise. See you in the spring, Dr. Curtis. Bye."

"Bye, Lisa."

As I went back to the lab, I wondered what Lisa's plans were for the holidays. She'd probably be with her husband in Frisco. I doubted if I would get another call from her. I kept thinking of her alluring body and seductive eyes; how could her husband not be happy with such a smart and great looking young woman? Hmm. Has he found someone else in San Francisco? Maybe Lisa discovered his infidelity? Oh, well, back to my samples. Now I had to get another woman out of my mind.

I finished another sample and put it in storage. It was 4:45; too late to dissolve another meteorite specimen. I packed two texts in my briefcase and locked up. The department office was nearly empty, except for Beth and the elderly physics professor, Gena Addario. She was talking to Beth about mailing something. I stuck my hand in my mailbox, but no new packages or letters today. That wasn't unusual for the afternoon; the early morning mail usually contained the museum packages. I took the stairs to the ground floor and stepped outside the building into bright sunlight and warmth. The air conditioning in the building was overactive; I almost needed a jacket indoors.

I had to squint as I looked for my red and white Pontiac. The sun's position was high enough above the horizon to make me wish I had a pair of clip-on shades. For some reason, I moved between my car and a gray SUV, but on the passenger side. When I got to the front of my car, someone called out to me.

"Hi, Dr. Curtis!"

I looked up momentarily to see one of my students from my Wednesday-Friday afternoon lecture class: Geology 311. As I waved and said, "Hi," I stepped on the concrete curb sticking out under the bumper and turned my ankle. The pain was sharp and extreme. All my weight had come down on the side of my foot. I knew I must have broken something. I hopped to the driver's side, unlocked the door, slid into the seat, and drove home. Ascending the stairs one at a time was painful. When inside, I cooked dinner walking on the heel of my left foot. As I ate, I knew I had to go to the hospital. If I took my shoe off, I probably wouldn't be able to put it on again due to swelling.

The main entrance of the hospital was locked, so I limped slowly to the emergency entrance behind the building. With every step I wondered why the emergency door was not on the side of the building, easily seen from the front. Why in God's name was it in the back? The architect probably had never gone to an emergency room himself. I wondered who had approved the building plans, probably a committee of townspeople.

There was a short chubby nurse inside, sitting in a plastic yard chair reading a magazine. She looked up, stood, and asked, "May I help you?"

"I sure hope so. I think I broke something in my left foot."

She dropped the magazine, quickly brought me a wheelchair and pushed me into ER 1.

"Are you in pain?"

All I thought was what a stupid question, but she was just doing her job.

"On a scale of 1 to 10, what would you estimate the pain to be?"

"Seven or eight." I winced when she wheeled the chair next to the bed. I noticed her name tag: Mary. Mary locked the wheels and told me to stand, turn ninety degrees, and sit on the bed. She didn't offer any assistance.

"You sit tight. I'm going to call the emergency room doctor. He should be here in a few minutes."

CHAPTER 14

MARY RETURNED pushing a portable x-ray machine. Still no doctor. Mary carefully removed my shoe and sock and two x-rays were taken: one from the top and one from the side. Ten more minutes of waiting and a doctor appeared. He resembled the archetypical army sergeant in street clothes with a stethoscope draped around his neck. He apologized for making me wait, but he had been called away from dinner to perform an emergency appendectomy which he had just completed. He spoke in a gentle manner. I immediately felt confident that he knew what he was doing.

Mary brought him the x-rays and he said, "Uh-huh. You've broken the 5th metatarsal. That's a bad one; a spiral fracture. Other than operate, we'll have to put a cast on your lower leg and give you some crutches." He patted my right knee and said, "Hang in there, I'll get my assistant to put your foot in a cast." He tapped my shoulder and said, "You're Dr. Curtis, right?"

I nodded. How would he know my name? He must have seen me at some function or perhaps my picture was in the newspaper as a new professor, but that would have been five years ago. I was impressed.

"I'm Dr. Mathew Mason. We'll take care of that break and get you home. Don't walk on it until tomorrow; use the crutches. How'd you get here?"

"I drove."

"Stick or automatic?"

"Automatic."

"Good. You can drive with one foot. Just be damn careful."

By the time the cast was on and they cut me loose from the emergency room, two hours of my lecture preparation time vanished.

I had planned on reading chapters from both texts before tomorrow's lectures, and I had to prepare a lecture for the minerology and crystallography class; I was least familiar with that material. It was my first time teaching that class and I hoped my lecture would come off as if I were better prepared.

As I finished the prep for the Geology 311 class, it suddenly struck me that I didn't need to prep a lecture for Willa's class; I could review for the first exam. I relaxed, had a cup of low-cal hot chocolate, watched the late news, and went to bed.

I woke up at 2:00 a.m., my foot hurting like hell. I had forgotten to take a pain pill before I went to bed. I hobbled to the bathroom in the dark, only about eight paces, took a pill, and sat to pee. I found my way back to bed using the wall as a guide, sat on the edge of the bed for a minute or so, tipped sideways, and went back to sleep. When the alarm sounded at 6:00 a.m., it took me a minute to figure out why I was on top of the sheet and blanket. I felt like I was in pretty good shape, my foot didn't hurt. That pill was magical.

After checking my blood glucose and taking my insulin, I had breakfast and put on my loosest pants. Getting my trouser leg over the cast was like trying to put on socks that were a couple of sizes too small, but I finally succeeded. If the cast had been any larger, I would have to have cut the left leg of my pants. I wondered if the physician's assistant knew my trouser size. Nah, it was just a matter of luck.

I finished dressing, shaved, and packed my briefcase. I thought I could manage the briefcase and the crutches, but it wasn't as easy as I had imagined. Fortunately, my hands were big enough to grasp the briefcase handle and the crutch handle together without too much stress on my fingers. When I got to my car, I knew I would have to switch hands holding the case and the crutch before getting to my office. My grip wasn't strong enough to last a long trek.

I took the elevator directly to the sixth floor. I skipped going by the departmental office to save my energy for longer journeys within the building. I leaned my crutches against the wall and unlocked my office door. With my briefcase on the floor, I shoved it with my crutches as I limped to my chair behind my desk and dropped into my chair. That's when I decided to turn my desk ninety degrees so it would be easier to sit down, but I'd need help to move the heavy furniture.

I sat in my chair, already as tired as I would normally have been at the end of the day. I must have been putting too much energy into walking with crutches. I never felt so out of shape. My hands and legs were ready for bed and the day had barely started. God bless the inventor of the elevator.

I remained at my desk working from my phone until 9:50 a.m. I was allotting myself an extra five minutes to get to class. I had to take the elevator; going down five flights of stairs was not an event I planned on taking again until I no longer wore the cast. According to the doctor, that meant about six weeks would elapse before my foot would be set free. The physician's assistant had instructed me to wait until Monday before I put my full weight on my left leg and foot. The walking cast needed time to harden. I figured by the time I got used to the crutches, I wouldn't need them. That turned out to be a naive notion.

I made it to my class with zero time to spare. As I somewhat clumsily entered the lecture hall, squeezing through the partially open door, I heard at least one audible gasp. I laid the crutches on the top of the bench at the front of the room and hopped to the lectern.

Someone asked, "What happened, Dr. Curtis?"

I smiled and said, "A wild driver ran over my foot."

Apparently no one believed me. Willa said, "What really happened?"

"It was a woman driver." I offered more information as a joke.

That got a big laugh, so I told them what I had done to myself. When I concluded, I said, "I apologize if I offended any of you ladies. I just thought the woman driver comment was mildly funny."

There was a slight stirring of voices, just background chatter, rustling, and then I said, "Your first exam will be a week from today. I've decided to review for the test today, but first, do any of you have questions?"

The next half-hour was spent answering questions about the lecture material and what type of questions would be on the exam. The following twenty minutes were spent with my quick review of previous lectures. I told the class I would briefly summarize any other pertinent subject matter on Monday and then move to new topics on Wednesday. I was closing my briefcase when a familiar voice asked, "Can I help you carry that back to your office? I've never used crutches before, but they seem awkward."

Willa's voice was unmistakable. I smiled and said, "That's a nice offer, I could use the assistance. I'm still learning how to work with these artificial supports."

She was beautiful today. She looked as if she had just come from a professional makeup artist's studio. I wished I had a camera. I'd have had a picture for my wallet.

She said, "You get your crutches and I'll get your briefcase."

As I swung the crutches into position, Willa said, "Are the test questions in here?" She lifted the case and laughed.

"Nope! You're thinking of swiping my briefcase to get the questions?" I grinned.

"Not really. You know I was just joking. I liked your comment about women drivers, even if it isn't true. The way you said it made it funny."

Willa held the door and I hopped twice to reach the three steps that went up to the hallway. "Please hold these things." I grabbed the railing with one hand and gave her the crutches. I hopped up the steps on my right leg and held out my hands for the crutches. She tipped them towards me and I adjusted my balance. The elevator was our next stop where she punched the up button and we waited for the doors to open. Willa waited for me to get in before stepping in beside me. We had the elevator to ourselves.

"You look very nice today. Are you going somewhere?"

"Thanks. I came to see you!"

I frowned and replied, "You're pulling my leg—not the one with the cast on it. You're going somewhere special today, aren't you?"

"Yeah. Steve and I have to go to a function at the base tonight. I'm not going to have time to get made up after I get home from classes, so I did it this morning."

"Well, you look terrific. I hope Steve appreciates you and your appearance. He's a lucky man."

"Thank you. I really don't want to go with him, but I guess it's my responsibility. The wives are supposed to get together to plan some functions scheduled for six months from now, after the men return from duty on the East Coast."

"You mean picnics? Things like that?"

"Probably." She exhaled slowly, "I'll make a potato salad, but I don't want to be in charge of anything. I've got enough to do with Peggy, school, and keeping the house clean. Most of the wives aren't taking classes; they just gossip a lot. I don't want to get into that rut."

I grinned, "Sounds like some of our faculty meetings."

When we arrived at my office door, Willa said, "I can't stay and talk today; maybe tomorrow. I have some questions for you—about the test material."

"Thanks for helping me back here. If you were a Girl Scout, I'd recommend a merit badge for you—invalid assistance."

She laughed and gave me a little wave. "Take care of your foot—see you tomorrow."

"Bye, Willa."

Damn, she looked good today. I couldn't imagine her husband not being happy with her. As soon as I was in my office the phone rang.

"Hello."

"Is this Dr. Curtis?"

"Yes."

"This is Nurse Amanda Tisor—from Dr. Mason's office. If you haven't begun walking on the cast, you may do so now. The cast should be hardened and will sustain your weight.

However, if the cast breaks, be sure to come in for repairs."

"All right. Thanks for the call."

I had expected the nurse to ask, "How are we doing today?" I was going to reply, "We are doing fine." I probably would have laughed, but it didn't happen, so I just grinned, went in the lab, and started processing another meteorite sample.

I worked on iron complexes all Tuesday morning. The cast didn't hamper my motions in the least and I worked very efficiently processing three more samples. Two more packages arrived in the mail and were brought to my office by a work study. I added the samples to the queue. After lunch, I worked on some test questions, had a mug of coffee and relaxed in my office chair for about fifteen minutes with my bum foot on top of my desk.

Willa arrived at exactly 1:00 p.m. I wasn't asleep, but I had closed my eyes for a few minutes, thinking about taking some samples to the mass spectroscopy lab, and imagining what the results would be. My office door was wide open and I heard someone come in and sit down. At least that is how I interpreted the few sounds I detected. I thought I'd take a guess.

"Hi, Willa." I opened my eyes and sat up straight, dropping my weighted leg to the floor.

"Oh! You scared me. I thought you were asleep."

"No. I was just thinking about my research. How are you today? How was that function you attended last night?"

"I'm tired. That meeting was really boring. Those wives wanted to know all about me, so I made up a few things for their entertainment."

I grinned and asked, "For example?"

"I told them I was born in jail. That kept them quiet for a few seconds, but then they wanted to know about school—all sorts of things. I told them I never went to school but I took the GED and qualified for college. Then they changed the subject. I think they weren't interested when they thought I wasn't educated like they were. Steve and I went home early. I was relieved to get out of there."

I had to laugh when she mentioned the jail episode, so I told her a true story. "My mother was really born in jail. Well, it wasn't a jail; it was the penitentiary in Washington State. My grandfather was in the Spanish American War and when he returned, he got a job as a guard at the prison. He and my grandmother lived in a cottage within the walls of the pen. After my mom was born, they moved to Yakima. That's why I laughed when you said you were born in a jail."

Willa's eyes sparkled, not unlike Lisa's, and her smile was warm and genuine. I felt very fortunate to have her as a student and friend and lucky to be able to talk so often to such a beautiful young woman. I found that we shared many of the same feelings and ideals. We talked for nearly the entire hour before she had to leave to pick up Peggy. No one else from the class had appeared to ask questions so we talked about the time after she moved from Moscow to Delight, Texas.

Willa had gained confidence in school and done very well until her junior year in high school. She fell under the spell of a senior boy and he used her for his amusement and pleasure. But she recovered after about a year, dropped out of school and worked at a carwash, a burger joint, and as a checkout at a grocery store. She met her husband, Steve, in Waco, and married him after a short courtship, in spite of her friends advising her otherwise. He was going into the Navy and she felt he would have a stable job for the foreseeable future. Steve had offered stability, relatively good wages, and opportunities for advancement in the service.

However, soon after Peggy was born, Willa realized she still had a desire to go to college, so she earned a GED and began taking a few college courses. That kept her interest when Steve was away from home. When he was stationed in the Philippines, she began having notions that he was not being faithful. Sometimes he would not return her calls, and when he did, she knew he was lying about his activities. She knew him much better than he realized.

Most of the talking was done by Willa during that hour we were together. I got the idea she was feeling relieved to have someone she trusted with whom she could share her past frustrations and relate her aspirations. I asked a few questions and tried to reinforce her past accomplishments and bolster her self-image. I told her several times that she was smarter than she thought, something I genuinely believed.

CHAPTER 15

FRIDAY PASSED quickly, except for the exam period. As I toured the room watching for cheaters, I kept glancing at Willa to see if I could determine if she might be having troubles, but she either didn't have any problems with the questions, or she was great at concealing difficulties.

I spent most of Saturday in the lab and graded exams Sunday afternoon and evening, taking an hour break for dinner and thirty minutes of TV news. When I completed the grading, I constructed a graph of scores versus frequency and made the letter grade assignments.

Willa received a 93, the top score, as I had hoped. I checked over her paper to make sure I hadn't given her any favorable treatment. The next scores were 91 and 89 then there was a six point gap to the next score, which was Gail Burnett's. I assigned the three high scores a letter grade of A. I was happy to see that Willa had done an excellent job. I hoped her high performance level would extend throughout the semester.

I returned the tests in random order on Monday. The students were a little wary of what they had accomplished, but I told them the average and the highest score and put the graphical display of the grades on the chalkboard. I could feel the tension in the room. When I gave Willa's test back, I said, "Good job, September." I gave similar comments to the other high scoring students. Following a few questions about my grading, I continued with lecture material.

Nearly every Tuesday and Thursday until Halloween, Willa came to my office for friendly chats. Occasionally, another student came by for help, but when some other student or students arrived, Willa left her books and exited my office. When the student left, Willa would reappear within a minute or so to continue our conversation. The third or fourth time this happened, I asked her where she went when she left my office.

"Once, I bought a candy bar from the machine and looked out the windows. A couple of times, I toured the building and used the ladies room. You know, if I weren't interested in geology, I think I'd take chemistry."

"Are you eligible for work-study?"

"I don't know. How would I find out?"

"The easiest way would be to ask Beth, the department secretary. She'll know where to apply—probably academic services in the administration building. I was thinking you could help me with my research. I'm doing chemical reactions involving numerous samples of meteorites. Each sample takes me an hour and I've got about a hundred more samples to run. I could use some help, but I don't want you to take time from something else that is important to you."

"Hmm. I sure could use the money. Christmas will be here before long. I'll find out and let you know." She smiled, glanced at her tiny wristwatch and said, "I've got to pick up Peggy. I'll see you next Tuesday, okay?"

"You won't be in class tomorrow?"

"No. I've got a doctor's appointment. Gail will take notes for me."

"I hope it's nothing serious."

"No. It's just a standard yearly visit—a wellness checkup. The navy doctors want to see if I'm still alive."

I hoped she would drop by again. The number of office hours remaining in the semester was rapidly diminishing. "I'll be here Saturday and Sunday. Have a nice weekend."

"Thanks. Bye." As she left my office, she turned quickly and waved before disappearing down the hall. I heard her hurried steps as she dashed to the elevators. She must have planned to pick up Peggy at a specific time and was worried about being late. I never saw her leave in such a rush before. I would have followed her out of my office doorway and watched her hurry down the hall, but the damn cast on my leg made me feel like I could only move in slow motion.

I prepared my Friday lectures during the time left in the afternoon so I wouldn't have to carry my briefcase home. Carrying a briefcase was awkward while still walking with crutches, trying not to put stress on my cast. I should have gotten a backpack, but I didn't want to go shopping when I was still dependent on the crutches. Besides, I would have to park some distance from a store that sold backpacks. I should have asked someone to get one for me, but it never occurred to me to ask—I was so used to doing things for myself. I disliked shopping for anything but groceries and it was an easily walk to the supermarket. I decided to leave my crutches home on the weekend.

I worked on meteorite samples all day Saturday, October 30, Halloween eve. On the way home, I bought a couple of packages of assorted small candy bars—individually wrapped pieces—for trick-or-treaters that might come by my apartment on Sunday. I didn't even try to go to the lab on Halloween; I decided to vegetate, listen to music, and think. When I had music playing I thought of Lisa and when I tried to think about my research, my thoughts were of Willa and Peggy. What was I going to do? I had no fantasy about instructions arriving from above.

After the sun went down, I could hear kids running around the nearby neighborhood. I turned out my lights and sat in the dark. I finally reached a conclusion concerning the two young women invading my thoughts. I had to take it calmly. How in my right mind could I simultaneously get involved with two beautiful young women when they were both married? Was I that starved for love? Was I a fool?

I heard tires crunching gravel in the parking lot below, but I concluded it was some of the other tenants or their guests. I didn't want to turn on my lights; that would draw kids to my door looking for candy. I felt a little like Scrooge. I'd eat the candy over a long period of time, a piece now and then, whenever I needed to raise my blood sugar. Then it happened. A knock on my door followed by a child's voice, "Twick or tweat."

Should I pretend there's no one home, or answer the door? I reluctantly made my way to the door, flipped the switch for the outdoor light, and opened the door. I was surprised by what I saw. Willa and Peggy were standing there in costume. "Trick or treat!" Willa was laughing—dressed as a pirate and Peggy was an angel or perhaps Tinker Bell, I couldn't tell.

"Hi! Come in. How did you find my place?" I turned on the inside lights, ushered them in, closed the door, and extinguished the porch light—no more visitors.

"We just looked for an apartment complex that fit the description you gave me several weeks ago."

"But you drove all this way for trick-or-treat? I don't understand." As soon as I said I didn't understand, Willa seemed to wilt a bit. "Where is Steve? Is he in the car?"

"No, he's in San Francisco for a week. A group from the base went there to get welding instructions—some new technique to speed up the repair process. Willa and I are on our own 'til Wednesday. I thought it would be a good time for a visit." She now seemed elated.

"Don't get me wrong, I'm happy you and Peggy came by. Would you like some coffee? I bought a new coffee maker and haven't used it much. I'm still in the experimental phase." I smiled. "You can be a guinea pig." I moved into the kitchen and started the coffee.

When my back was turned Willa said, "You're calling me a pig?"

I hesitated, holding a scoop of coffee. I glanced at her and saw the biggest grin I had ever seen. I thought of a quick answer.

"Nope. You are the most beautiful woman I have ever known."

"That's a bunch of blarney, and I'm not Irish, but I know it when I hear it."

"It's true Willa. You don't know how pretty you are, even in disguise." I looked at Peggy, who had crawled up on my sofa. "You are a beautiful fairy, Peggy." She just looked at me and then at Willa.

"Tell him you're an angel, Peg."

Peggy spoke slowly and quietly, as if she were embarrassed, "I'm an angel."

"Oh. I thought you were a pixie or a fairy, but I was wrong. You are a beautiful angel. Where did you get your costume?"

"Mommy made it." She looked at Willa and grinned.

While the coffee was perking, we talked about her costume making and her crazy facial makeup. She had made scars on her forehead with an eyebrow pencil and her left eye was blackened as if covered with a patch.

She explained, "I didn't want to use an actual eyepatch, it would hamper my driving."

I grinned and replied, "Oh, I thought you might be fifty percent raccoon."

Fortunately, Willa laughed. She pointed at Peggy. Peggy was curled up and had fallen asleep on the couch.

I made my way over to see her better and remarked, "She is really cute, Willa. You're going to have to keep the boys away, but you know about that." Willa didn't comment, but stood and walked into the kitchen, got two mugs from the cupboard and poured the coffee. Her knowing where I kept things surprised me a little, but the glasses and mugs were in a logical place above and to the left of the sink.

We talked for about ten minutes. I noticed she just sipped a small amount of her coffee.

I smiled, "I see you like my coffee."

She sat back in her chair and pushed the mug away with both hands. "It's terrible! You need more practice. That stuff could be for cleaning used bricks."

We both started laughing and I apologized. "Maybe I'll do better some other time."

"I hope so." She looked at her watch, got up and said, "We'd better go. It will take me thirty minutes to get home. Tomorrow is a school day, you know." She smiled and moved toward Peggy and scooped her up.

"I wish I could help you with Peggy, but I don't want to risk falling on the stairs. Can you carry her all right?"

She nodded and said, "Oh, yeah. I'm stronger than I look, Ned."

I moved as quickly as I could to get to the door. If she hadn't been carrying Peggy I would have tried to kiss her, but on second thought, I couldn't risk not seeing her again except in class. But I did wonder how she would have reacted. No one would have seen us. As she descended the stairs, I said, "Drive carefully. See you in the morning."

"Bye, Ned. Get some rest."

I closed the door and listened as the dark-green station wagon pulled out of the parking lot. It was too late for any more coffee, so I disposed of the remainder. I laughed as I poured it down the kitchen sink drain. According to Willa, I wouldn't need a drain cleaner for some time.

I sat at the kitchen table for a few minutes thinking about Willa and Peggy. Willa had expended a significant amount of effort to locate my apartment. What was her goal? It couldn't be brownnosing. She didn't need to do that; she was too damn smart. What did she see in me? Was I a father figure? I was almost old enough to be her father, but she appeared to have a significant concern for my welfare. Was I making more of her actions and words than they warranted? I couldn't help being attracted to such a gorgeous young woman.

I moved into the living room and reviewed for Monday's lecture. After twenty minutes, I was ready. If I got to the lab early enough, I could work up another meteorite sample before class. Clean clothes for Monday were laid out on the top of the clothes hamper, and after showering, I climbed into bed. Climbing was an appropriate description; the cast created discomfort that I had never experienced before. Eventually, I found relief by propping my left leg and cast on a pillow under a sheet and blanket. I lay there thinking until midnight when I said a short prayer for Willa's and Peggy's safe trip home, although by that time they were probably already in bed. The next thing I became aware of was the sound of my alarm.

I rarely used the snooze button, but I tapped the clock with my fingers. Ten minutes later I uncovered my cast and swung out of bed before trudging into the kitchen and making a pot of coffee that was tolerable. Another attempt at the coffee would probably yield even better results. I still didn't have the water to coffee ratio correct for my palate—antacid tablets were still necessary.

As I gave my ten o'clock lecture, I noticed Willa and Gail occasionally whispering but I didn't see any smiles or other facial expressions from either woman. I guessed they were talking about the lecture material. I didn't see Willa again until Tuesday at one o'clock. I was in the lab and had just finished filtering a small crop of red crystals when Willa appeared in my office. I routinely kept my office door to the lab wide open so I could hear the phone and see if I had any visitors. I looked at her and said, "I'll be right with you, have a seat." I rinsed my hands and joined her.

"How was your trip home Sunday night?"

"Peggy slept all the way. I listened to a talk-show most of the way. Someone called in about the meteor, but the host hadn't heard anything more about it. I felt like telling them you could answer all their questions, but I didn't have a phone."

"Interesting. I've never done talk-radio. I wonder what I would sound like."

"You have a very calming voice. You always sound like you know what you're talking about. You would be a good guest on one of those shows."

"Thanks, but I'd probably put my foot in my mouth—the right one." I smiled.

Willa laughed, understanding the expression, but knowing my left foot was covered with a plaster cast. "I know what you mean, I've put my foot in my mouth before. It can be pretty embarrassing."

She noticed two small packages on my desk and asked, "Christmas gifts?"

"Kind of. Open one and see what it is."

She frowned, picked up the top parcel and shook it.

I laughed, "It doesn't rattle."

She smiled and pointed it at me. "You already shook it?"

"Nope, but I know what it is."

"X-ray vision?" She smiled. "It's something you ordered?"

"No, it's a gift of sorts." I decided to explain as she tore off the wrapping. "It's a sample of a meteorite—from outer space."

She hesitated. "Is it radio-active?"

"Not that I know of. It's made of iron."

"Oh." She nodded, "It's for your research."

I smiled and nodded, "That's right."

She opened the cardboard carton and withdrew a small container the size of a jewelry box that in a movie would contain an engagement ring. She looked questioningly at me.

"Go ahead, open it."

Willa slowly lifted the lid and peered inside the little container. She pulled out a small plastic bag that held a bean-sized piece of meteorite. We started laughing as she held up the little bag like it smelled bad.

I asked, "Where's it from?"

Willa looked at the wrapping paper and read the return address, "Millinocket, Maine. I've never heard of that place."

I responded, "Me either. I don't remember talking to anyone from there. Maybe one of the bigger city museums asked them to send me a sample. I'll probably get a letter from them before long."

"Oh, I have some bad news. I can't get work-study until next semester. Something about regulations—but I can work for you next spring if you like."

"Great! I'll still have plenty to do. Hopefully, you'll be able to put in an hour a day, or three hours a week; something like that. Whatever you can fit into your busy schedule."

"They told me there's a limit on hours—so the work doesn't interfere with studies. Makes sense. I'll have to work out a schedule when I know my classes and know what your teaching assignment is."

"Well, I can have Beth let you in to work if I'm not in my office."

Willa sat back and looked disappointed but I would feel the same way or even more so. I just didn't let it show. I wanted her to know that she could get her hours in, even if I wasn't in my office. I had no idea what her financial situation was. Did she need the money, or did she want to come in to share her thoughts with me, or both? I really enjoyed her company and I hoped she felt the same way.

CHAPTER 16

O N MONDAY, a few days before Thanksgiving, Willa dropped by my office early in the morning. Her untimely appearance was a pleasant surprise. Ordinarily, she would drop by at my scheduled office hours on Tuesday and Thursday. Her visits had become regular events. She just dropped off Peggy at the children's center and was on her way to take an exam. I noticed her uneasiness and asked, "Are you all right?"

She hesitated a moment and said, "I just wanted you to know that I wish I could ask you over for Thanksgiving, but it's too complicated. My husband wouldn't understand and I don't want him knowing about us when I was a kid, he would only have more ammunition when we argue. Our recent arguments have been happening more often than before. I'm not sure why, but maybe he suspects there is someone else in my life."

"Has Peggy mentioned anything about me? She seemed to have fun with the molecular model set and she saw me at Halloween."

"No. She wouldn't remember that. She's too excited about going to school with me so she can attend the activity center. The students treat the kids like royalty—she loves it there."

"Sounds like it's a lot better than leaving her with a sitter."

"Oh, for sure. She talks about it all the time. Well, I'd better go. I've got to cram for a few minutes before the test."

"Good luck, although you probably don't need it. And about Thanksgiving; thanks for thinking of me, but one of the biology professors invited me over for dinner with his family. I dread the thought that they might ask me to say grace."

Willa looked puzzled. She frowned and cocked her head to the side, expecting me to elaborate.

I explained, "Except for a couple of weddings, I've only been in a church once since being confirmed as a Methodist when I was twelve. I know very little about religion and feel uncomfortable when people quote verses from the Bible."

"Well, I think they're just being nice since you live alone. Well, I've got to go. See you in class." She turned and ran to the elevator. She must have been a good athlete when younger and had kept in great shape, an obvious conclusion to any man that checked out women.

The next exam in Willa's class came the week after Thanksgiving. She scored in the 90s again, but just barely, a 91. One student had a higher grade. His name was Rick Strand. Rick was a little older than my regular students and had a family. I was pleased to see the more mature students doing so well in class.

The remainder of the semester: two days of November, and three weeks of December, flew by seemingly in record time. Final exams were given on the nineteenth through the twenty-second. Following her last final, Willa came by and gave me a present. The box was wrapped with red- and green-plaid Christmas paper with little Santa Claus figures and Teddy bears spread randomly on all sides. There was a big bow, made from white ribbon, on one side with a gift tag attached beneath the fancy ribbon. It said, To: Dr. Ned. From: Willa and Peggy. I couldn't figure out what was in the box; it didn't rattle and was fairly heavy.

"Thank you very much, Willa. I have something for you, too, but it's not much." I had ordered a T-shirt with a Geologic Society Emblem for Willa. I thought it wouldn't cause any suspicion from her husband. It was for the student with the highest grade average in Willa's class, but I had decided to give it to Willa even if she didn't have the highest grade. I had stuck a red bow on the white box it had come in so it looked festive. I attached a tag explaining the award. It had cost me fifteen dollars but was a good quality shirt—something to wear at a barbeque or at home. I hadn't thought it would accentuate her figure, but it did. She opened it in my office and put it over her loose fitting blouse. The fit was a little tight. She looked damn sexy in it.

"Thank you, Ned." Willa pointed at the gift she had brought me "Don't open your present 'til Christmas."

"Okay." I smiled, "I think you'd better take off the T-shirt, it might shut off the blood flow to your brain and increase the blood flow in your male classmates."

We both laughed and wished each other a Merry Christmas.

After taking my medication and putting two slices of bread in the toaster on Christmas day, I opened Willa's gift; I followed her request. It was a picture of a winter scene of Bretton Woods, New Hampshire.

Willa must have remembered what I said about wanting to build a mountain cabin near trees and a stream. Trees dusted with snow, and the partially iced over stream were prominent in the print with a mountain range in the background. She had picked out a beautiful picture for me. I think she remembered the bare walls of my apartment when she brought Peggy by on Halloween.

I had considered getting her some jewelry, not going overboard, but just something nice; something a friend might give as a present. However, Willa wouldn't have been able to explain that to her husband. I thought the T-shirt was my only option.

The week from Christmas to New Years was a busy time for me in the lab. I decided to take my transistor radio to work and listen to classical music in the background as I toiled. The departmental mail was delivered during the holidays and I received ten more packages containing thirty-one samples. I wanted to process all the meteorite samples but only accomplished a little more than half my goal—twenty-one specimens were converted to the red complex. I had accumulated fifty-three samples to submit to the mass spec lab when it was scheduled to resume operation on January 4, 1988.

Once I had that data, I would have many hours of sorting and mulling over the resulting numbers. I had to make sure I didn't transpose any of the figures, so I was looking forward to Willa's help checking the iron isotope ratios. The project was becoming more tedious than I had originally expected, but that was typical of many of the research articles I was examining; I could read between the lines and detect the investigators' waning enthusiasm; they were looking forward to the conclusion. Hopefully, something of significance would result from my study of the meteorites—worthy of publication in a reputable journal.

On January 2 the doldrums hit, so I decided to drive around and see if I could find something interesting that would keep me from continuing to scold myself for not working on more samples during the Christmas break. I was driving eastbound along highway 76 and saw a sign giving the distance to Palomar Mountain. Lisa's image flashed through my mind and I reached in my shirt pocket. There it was: the directions to Lisa's quarters on Mt. Palomar. I hoped she hadn't gone anywhere for the holidays, so I continued on to the observatory.

I took county road S6 and wound my way through the mountainous terrain to the observatory gates. The visitor parking lot was nearly deserted, but I saw a sign that stated the gates would be locked at 4:00 p.m. Pacific Daylight Time; overnight parking was not permitted.

Since the lot contained only one other vehicle, there was plenty of space to park. I locked my car and followed the foot path toward the telescope and deviated to the right to the Visitor Center. Hopefully, I would see another human being; someone that knew the whereabouts of graduate students. Lisa's directions were not very specific except for getting to the observatory.

I entered the Gift Shop where I found a middle-aged woman sitting behind a counter reading *Hollywood Profiles,* not *Astronomy*, as I had expected. She looked up and stood as I approached. "Elaine" was embroidered in cursive on her name tag.

"May I help you?"

I don't think she expected anyone, the place seemed nearly deserted. I recognized a slight Spanish accent. "Yes. I'm looking for a friend of mine, Lisa Landers. She's a graduate student."

"Oh, yes. I know Lisa. But she isn't here now. She left to visit someone in San Francisco. She told me she would be back Friday, January 6. Do you want to leave her a message?"

"No—well, yes. Tell her Ned Curtis stopped to see her and get a tour of the observatory. I'm sorry I missed her."

"All right, I'll tell her you stopped by. Can I ask what you do, Mr. Curtis?"

"I'm an assistant professor of geology at Ocean Vista University."

"Oh! You are Doctor Curtis she talked about. She will be disappointed."

"Thank you for taking my message. I think I'll start back; the weather report on the radio said it might snow on the mountain tonight. Goodbye."

"Goodbye, Dr. Curtis. Have a safe trip." She smiled and gave a slight hand wave.

"Thank you, Elaine." I grinned and headed for the door.

Exiting the Visitor Center, I felt the chill in the air and the slight breeze for the first time. When I had arrived at the parking lot, I hadn't even noticed the frigid weather. I think I had been anticipating seeing Lisa and hadn't noticed the cool air. I unlocked and climbed into my car for shelter. I donned my Nylon field jacket which would suffice to preserve body heat until the car warmed up. As I drove back down the mountain road, I wondered what Lisa and Elaine had talked about. I'll probably never know, but maybe Lisa will tell me sometime. It was probably something very innocent. Perhaps Lisa had mentioned my name when talking about the meteor crater we visited in Death Valley. Maybe she'll stop by my office once the new semester starts; she said she would.

Registration took place on January 4, 5, and 6. On the fourth, I was slightly perturbed when I discovered I wasn't assigned to teach the second semester beginning geology class. For some unknown reason, Dr. Reynolds assigned himself to the class and I was to teach his upper division course: Geology 463, Stratigraphy. That was going to require more preparation time on my part. I had never taught the course before. I was puzzled at the assignment; Geology 463 was his favorite class. I wondered what had influenced Reynold's decision.

I advised about a dozen students during registration and the interruptions to my lab work prevented me from processing as many samples as I would have liked. Most of the consultations took only fifteen minutes or less, but that was enough to slow my work to a crawl. By Friday, I was looking forward to seeing Willa again. It had been two weeks since we had last talked. Friday came and went. Willa had not come to see me. I wondered if she was all right.

I was surprised Saturday afternoon. I had locked my door so I could do lab work without intrusion, but there was a rap on my door. I said, "Damn!" But then I thought it might be Willa, so I went to investigate. It was Lisa.

The pretty face displayed an enormous smile and her eyes had that twinkle I couldn't resist. That sparkle had an almost hypnotic effect on me. She was dressed in a pink sweater, black slacks, and heels. What a knockout! She almost took my breath away. I stifled a "Wow!"

"Lisa! How are you?"

"I'm great, Dr. Curtis. I have something for you." She handed me a package that appeared to contain an article of clothing. It was light and soft, wrapped in Christmas paper. I was perplexed but accepted the gift.

"Merry Christmas! I wanted to give it to you earlier, but I had to visit my husband in Northern California. I got back yesterday, talked to Elaine, and had to come see you. Brian and I have separated." She reached out, took my hand, and gave it a squeeze.

"Thank you for the present, but I don't have anything for you. I hope you didn't spend much money on it. Come in, come in. I'm sorry, my manners are terrible. Living alone doesn't prepare one very well for normal etiquette." I led her into my office to Willa's chair. I sat on the edge of my desk, still holding her hand.

"Oh, I didn't expect you to get me anything. I made your gift in my spare time. I remembered you saying you wished you had one of those Russian fur hats for your fall and winter excursions in the mountains. Open it and try it on." Her eyes were glistening and I had to look away from her at the package to avoid thinking of what lay under her clothing.

I started to untie the ribbon, but she couldn't wait. "Just rip it open! Don't try to save the paper."

As I tore the package open, I asked, "So you talked with Elaine at the observatory?"

"Uh-huh." She smiled, her eyes dancing. "She's really a nice lady. Elaine has been like a mother to me. She tells me which guys to stay away from. She thinks I need help to find a man that will respect me."

"What did she think of me?" I grinned, not expecting an answer.

"She liked you, but she said I should be careful of professors."

I cocked my head a little to the side and grinned. "I've never bitten anyone but my sister when we were kids.."

"That's not what worries her, Dr. Curtis."

"You can call me Ned, Lisa. I'm not one of your professors. We can be on a first name basis, unless that makes you uncomfortable."

"No, I'd like that."

"Can I take you somewhere to eat? It's about time for dinner."

She gave me a suspicious grin, "At your place?"

I laughed and replied, "No. I don't have anything in my refrigerator that I could offer you to eat. The expiration date has lapsed on most of my stuff. We could go to McDonalds or Dairy Queen for a burger."

"Okay. I can't stay very long anyway. I don't like driving to the observatory at night. That mountain road is dangerous, especially with patches of snow and ice. There was a storm a couple of days ago."

"Let me shut down my lab and then we'll go. You can drive."

Lisa was driving a black VW beetle. I squeezed in front with her. My long legs forced my knees against the dash, but in five minutes we were at McDonalds. I had a cheeseburger and a diet coke and she ordered a salad and coffee. We talked about her classes and her research project and I explained what I had done on my project since the trip to the meteor crater.

Lisa was a polished conversationalist. We discussed music, religion, astronomy, geology, and several other topics before I reminded her of the time. She had to start back.

CHAPTER 17

A S WE drove back to the Physical Sciences Building, we shared some jokes and had a few good laughs. Lisa had picked up a few jokes during her astronomical studies and I could see she enjoyed passing them on to me. She thanked me for dinner and let me out next to my car. As her VW left the parking lot, she beeped the horn twice, and I watched her little black beetle turn and head for the highway. I hadn't enjoyed a cheeseburger that much in years.

I spent Sunday working on lectures for my stratigraphy class. I decided each Sunday would be devoted to preparing three lectures for the next week. Although I essentially copied Dr. Reynold's syllabus, I altered some of the exercises to follow material I was more familiar with rather than depend on his background strengths. I thought the class should be made more aware of isotopic stratigraphy instead of depending almost entirely on lithostratigraphy. I felt more comfortable with my approach than with Dr. Reynold's method. Much of the first few lectures would be spent giving examples and defining terms to be used during the semester.

Dr. Reynold's assigning me a lighter teaching load than usual was much appreciated. He recognized that I needed time to complete my research and publish the findings. Apparently he wanted me to stay on. Then I had another thought; he might not have wanted to recruit another assistant professor to replace me. Interviewing prospective candidates was not a pleasant experience, especially from the point of view as head of the committee. I still wondered why he had assigned me to teach his favorite course. I needed to talk to his wife; I'm sure she would know his thoughts. I hoped I wouldn't be treading on haloed ground.

Monday morning brought the excitement of the first day of the spring semester to the whole campus. As I walked cautiously from my car to the building, I could hear the enthusiasm in the voices of the students I passed on the sidewalk. It had been a month since I had my cast removed, but I was still aware of the atrophy of my left leg muscles, especially the calf.

I stopped by the departmental office on the way to the sixth floor. When I reached into my mailbox, Beth said, "Dr. Curtis, Mrs. Reynolds wants to speak to you. She's in my office."

I turned around and said, "Good morning, Beth. Mrs. R is here?"

Beth nodded and motioned for me to follow her, so I stepped between the two office desks and trailed a few paces to her office. Beth's office door was closed; she knocked on the frosted glass window and we entered the small room. Gloria was sitting with her hands clasped around her purse on her lap. She looked up at me, started to stand, but decided to remain seated.

"Please be seated, Dr. Curtis. I need to tell you something. It's important."

I frowned, but said, "Hi Gloria, how are you?"

"I'm fine, thank you. It's about Ethan."

I could see tears forming in her eyes and she looked away at the floor. "He's got Alzheimer's and can't teach any longer." She hesitated as I absorbed what she had said, "He just can't do it anymore."

I moved a chair closer and sat beside her. Beth closed the door and went back to her outer desk, leaving us alone. I held one of her hands with mine and asked, "What can I do to help?"

Tears were streaming down her cheeks now. I pulled out my handkerchief and offered it to her. She blotted her face and answered, "You'll have to take over his second semester beginning class. Dr. Telloc is taking his other three-hour and the seminar. I'm so sorry about this. I know you need time to work on your research. Ethan and I discussed this last summer—before he began to have so much trouble. His memory is failing and he gets confused easily now."

"Don't worry about me, Gloria. You take care of Ethan. He needs you now, more than ever."

"Oh, thank you, I hoped you would understand. His class starts at nine o'clock; can you be ready?"

"Sure, I'll throw something together. Did he have a syllabus made up for the class?"

"I asked him that last week and he didn't know what I was talking about. That's when I knew he couldn't carry on. We saw his doctor and he said no to teaching. I thought it would bother him, but he didn't seem to care. I called the president of the university and he recommended that I ask you to take over his duties temporarily. Dr. Ardmore has full confidence in you."

"So, I am the acting department chair?" I had no idea what to do next.

"It will only be for a couple of weeks. Dr. Ardmore is going to have Dr. Larson in chemistry take over for the rest of the year. Bob Larson has a strong background in geology. He'll start the search for Ethan's replacement."

"Boy, you had me scared for a minute. Thanks for telling me about Dr. Larson. I'll consult with him about any pending matters."

Gloria looked so disheartened sitting there with her hands clasped over her purse. She didn't seem to be overwhelmed, but she occasionally mumbled something as she stared at her hands. I couldn't help but feel sorry for what she was going to experience as Ethan began sliding further downhill mentally and physically. I couldn't think of anything compassionate to say; the revelation had taken me by surprise. I noticed Beth's wall clock and realized I had less than thirty minutes to get ready for class, not enough time to generate a new syllabus. I'd have to tell the students the course outline would be ready on Wednesday.

I stood and said, "I'd better go now, Gloria. Thanks for telling me about your husband and my best wishes for you and Ethan. I'll keep in touch. Bye for now."

"Thank you, Ned. I'm sorry to have to pile this on you. Good luck with your teaching load and I hope you can get your research completed—in spite of the pinch in time. Bye."

My mind shifted from the Reynolds' problems to the short time I had to get ready for class. I took the elevator and walked as quickly as possible to my office. I still favored my left foot and couldn't run, although I wanted to. Fortunately, I could continue in the text where I had left off at the end of fall semester.

I scanned Chapter 14 and hurriedly jotted down a few notes. I was getting the first day jitters and had to calm down. There was nothing I could do at the last minute to make this upcoming nine o'clock lecture anything admirable; I would just have to wing it. I made a pot of coffee, poured the steaming java in my usual ceramic mug and set off for class. If I took the stairs, I thought I should be calmed down by the time I got to the lecture room. I would be worrying more about my foot than the upcoming unprepared-for class.

It was 8:57 when I entered the room. There was a lull in the student conversations when they saw me. I saw Willa sitting with Gail, but in a different location than last semester. They were in the second row left of the center aisle. The class was slightly smaller than I expected, but I saw most of the faces I had gotten used to in the fall. As I scanned the expectant expressions, I was pleased to see the abundance of smiles, especially from Willa and Gail.

I addressed the class, "I know you were expecting Dr. Reynolds, but you're going to have to put up with me for another semester." There was some applause, the most exuberant coming from Gail and Willa, before a young man asked, "Is Dr. Reynolds sick?"

I didn't quite know how to answer that question. I wasn't sure Gloria Reynolds wanted people to know about Professor Reynolds having dementia. But they would find out soon enough, so I said, "He has Alzheimer's and is no longer teaching. It was a surprise—I just found out about it this morning." I glanced at the wall clock, "About an hour ago."

I promised to get them a syllabus on Wednesday and began a short lecture on what I believed would be covered during the semester. We wouldn't cover the entirety of the remaining chapters but I would only omit material that could be read and understood without my assistance. The class seemed to accept my plan. I dismissed the students after thirty minutes.

The entire class, except for one student, rushed out of the room as if we were having a fire drill. Willa slowly packed her things in a backpack and came down to the lectern smiling.

"I received work-study for spring semester. Do you still want me to work for you?"

"More than ever now that I have another course to teach. That sounds great. How many hours did they give you?"

"I'm limited to twenty per month. Is that going to be enough to help you get your project completed?"

"With your brains and assistance in my lab, I should be able to complete my research project with time to spare. You're going to be a big help."

"I sure hope so. I sensed your disappointment that Dr. Reynolds wasn't going to be teaching any longer. Was that your only reason for disappointment?"

"No. Some of it was selfish. I was supposed to have a smaller teaching load so I could get my research completed, but now my teaching load is bigger than normal." I gave Willa a sour look, but then I smiled. "Now that you're on work-study, it will cancel out some of the stress of the large teaching load. You've made my day. Can I buy you a cup of coffee?"

She grinned, "Ah, your coffee?"

I laughed with her and said, "No. We'll go to the student center, unless you don't want to be seen with me."

"What? Why would you think that?" There was a trace of annoyance in her voice.

"If we're seen together, you'll be accused of brown-nosing. It might get back to your husband that you were having coffee with some old dude."

"He's on the East Coast. Nobody but Gail knows about you and she won't say anything."

"Okay. Let's go!" As we walked to the student center, I hoped a faculty member would see me with a pretty young lady and spread the information to the ladies of the academic social society of gossipmongers. Mrs. Reynolds would be pleased to know I wasn't gay, or at least I would begin building some evidence.

As Willa and I moved along the cafeteria counter, I asked, "Want a doughnut or a sweet roll? I'm buying."

"I'd better not, but thanks. I'm trying to maintain my figure." She eyed the doughnuts and licked her lips. She looked at me and pretended to hide behind her notebook.

"You don't need to worry about that. You look great. I can't imagine you being fat."

She asked, "Have you always been thin?"

"I've weighed around 180 for the last ten years. I lose a little during the academic year and gain it back during the summer—when I'm not stressed out." I paid for our drinks and we moved toward a table, but Willa said, "Let's go to your office. I'm more comfortable there."

That was fine with me. I had another class at 10:00 a.m. so I wasn't going to have to run to my office, pick up my book and notes, and hurry to class.

As we entered the science building, Broman Hall, Willa commented, "You're still favoring your left leg, aren't you?"

I nodded. "Uh-huh. I sleep with a sock on my left foot." I winked, "A bit of a security blanket. I worry a little that I might stub my little toe if I get up at night. I can't afford to break that bone again. I have some pain when I walk, but it's not bad enough to even bother with an aspirin. I don't like taking pills."

Two other people got on the elevator with us. They got off on the fourth floor and we continued to the sixth. Willa sat in her usual chair now at the side of my desk and shrugged out of her light jacket. I had my desk rotated during the holidays so I sat down at a right angle to her and took a sip of my still steaming coffee.

I leaned back and said, "Ah, that's good beer."

She grinned and set her coffee on the edge of my desk. "Now that we're alone, would you like to come to dinner on Saturday? Peg and I will be serving spaghetti and meatballs and a salad."

"Homemade?"

She laughed and replied, "No. I'm having it flown in from Italy."

I grinned. "That's why you didn't want to ask me at the student center. It's a big deal and you didn't want anyone else to know about it. I was wondering why you wanted to come to my office. I thought you just wanted to ride the elevator. Well, don't have wine sent along. I don't drink."

Fortunately, Willa was now laughing. She had a great laugh. There were so many things to like about her. I couldn't imagine why her husband was such a bastard. I imagined that he treated all women with disdain.

She looked at her watch and said, "You've got a class in ten minutes and so do I." She stood to leave. "Oh! Can I start working this afternoon?"

"Sure. Can you be here at one o'clock? I'll show you the lab procedure and you can process some samples while I start working on the data I've collected."

"Okay. See you at one." As she moved toward the door, she pointed at her coffee and commented, "You can have what's left. It's still hot. It's much better than your home brew." She gave a slight giggle and disappeared down the hall.

I used a couple of minutes to review my notes and headed to class on the second floor. I expected a small group of around eight students. According to the class list, seven geology majors were enrolled in the stratigraphy course, but usually the final number of enrollees was one or two greater. I was mildly shocked when I got to class; there were thirteen students present.

There was a hush when I entered the lecture room. I scanned the expectant faces and took a look at the roll sheet. I recognized a few faces and names, but there were some unfamiliar students also. I had to question the group. "Can anyone tell me why the class is this big? I thought there would be seven or eight students."

A young man sitting in back answered, "We heard you were teaching the class."

I wanted to grin but hesitated for a moment and then said, "Dr. Reynolds has dementia and has retired from teaching. I just found out about it this morning. I'm telling you because there will probably be rumors. Alzheimer's is something one does not recover from. Dr. Reynolds and his wife consulted with the president and decided he should retire. If you hear strange rumors floating about, tell them the truth."

I left it at that and passed out the syllabus. "I'd like this class to be one of participation. I hope you come to class prepared so we can get some good discussion flowing. If any of you are afraid to talk in this small group, don't worry about it. By the end of the semester, you will have the confidence and knowledge to teach the class—with a little assistance from a professor."

I pointed at myself and got a few chuckles. "If any of you are afraid to speak up in class, don't run off and withdraw until you have at least come to class for one week." I surveyed the class and there were no questions. "Okay, that's it for today. Come prepared for discussion on Wednesday. Please have at least one question ready; it doesn't have to be earth shattering."

Willa was prompt. When I opened my door after eating lunch, she was standing in front of me ready to knock on my door. We both grinned and she marched into my office, deposited her books on her chair and went straight into the lab.

"Show me what to do and I'll get to work. We've got to get your research finished so you don't get fired."

I was a little surprised at how aggressive she was concerning my work, but I was also pleased with her interest in saving my job. Rather than explain the procedures, I suggested she take notes as I processed a sample. We spent over an hour on the sample because I had to explain why I was following the routine so closely. Willa's questions were not trivial; she had caught on very rapidly and even suggested some things

I found difficult to ignore. I therefore altered my procedure slightly but was sure the change wouldn't influence the results.

When the sample had been stored and labelled, Willa left to pick up Peggy and head for home. I was sorry to say goodbye, but she said, "See you tomorrow. Have a nice evening."

I replied, "You, too, Willa. Tell Peggy hi for me and be careful on your way home. Bye."

CHAPTER 18

THAT FIRST week of spring semester classes seemed to pass very quickly. Time flies when busy. When Willa and I were working Friday afternoon, she gave me a sheet of paper from her three-ring binder with directions to her home. The spaghetti dinner was Saturday.

"When do you want me to come over?"

"I know you eat at five, so any time after four would be fine. It takes about twenty minutes to get to my place from the campus."

"All right. I'll be there a little after four o'clock—if I don't get lost."

She shook her head and grinned, "Just follow my directions; you won't get lost."

I showered and shaved early Saturday afternoon, splashed on some Old Spice aftershave and then decided I had overdone it. I washed my face with a little water and dried off. I judged the residual aftershave fumes were about right. I didn't want to stink up Willa's home. It was 3:50 when I left my apartment and headed to Del Mar on Highway 15. Without Willa's map, I would have been lost for at least an hour, but I followed directions exactly. It took me twenty-five minutes to find her house.

It was on a side road almost hidden behind some trees and a large sign advertising sail boats. I made a left turn at the sign and drove about a quarter mile before I reached a neighborhood of small homes. I watched for number 2911 and spotted it after making a right hand turn to a second street parallel to the one that brought me to the area. I parked behind Willa's green station wagon on a blacktop driveway not far from the front door.

I hadn't thought to ask her if I could bring something, but at the last minute I had picked up some apples, oranges, and a gigantic jar of peanut butter. I figured those items could be used at any time. Flowers would have been too much, but what did I know? I hadn't been on a date in nearly eight years. I carried the groceries to the entrance and rapped three times on the screen door.

I heard Willa's voice through the screen. "Peggy, please go to the door and invite the man in."

I couldn't see far into the house through the wire mesh; the front door faced east and the sun was hanging over the ocean, but wouldn't set until about six o'clock, in nearly two hours. The vertical blinds on the western windows were closed. It almost looked like the inside of a theater; the light inside was dim and my eyes were accustomed to the bright outdoors.

Peggy came to the door and had trouble turning the lever to open the screen. I pressed the button on the latch and Peggy pushed the screen door open. "Mommy said you can come in."

"Thank you, Peg. I have some things for you and your mom."

I was about ten feet from a small oval kitchen table that would accommodate four adults with some difficulty, maybe two adults and two children would be less cramped. I placed the fruit on a large plate on the counter next to the sink and the peanut butter jar next to the fruit. I tossed the empty sack in the waste basket under the sink; the door on the cabinet under the sink was missing.

"Hi, Ned!" I turned around to see Willa in a white blouse, black skirt, black heels, and sheer nylons. I felt a little out of place; I was not suitably dressed if we were going out.

"Wow! You look terrific! I should have worn a coat and tie. You look very classy."

She did a little curtsy and said, "Thank you. It's the first time I've ever had a professor over for dinner. Do you think I've overdone it?"

I thought she had, but I didn't want to embarrass her. "No. But you'd better wear an apron so you don't get spaghetti sauce on your clothes." I grinned, but I couldn't take my eyes off her. She had put on just the right amount of makeup; it didn't take much— she looked terrific.

"You can help me set the table. The salad is in the fridge. You get it and I'll get the spaghetti." She was keeping the pasta warm in the oven. "Peggy, can you put the plates on the table?"

I placed the salad bowl in the center of the table and reached over to help Peggy with the three large plates.

"No! I want to." I jerked my hands back and stepped away from the table. She was in charge. She was able to get the plates from the countertop when she was on her tiptoes. I was afraid she might drop them, but she handled the plates one at a time without any trouble.

I said, "Good job, Peggy. You didn't need any help after all." She smiled and opened the silverware drawer, picked out three forks, and three knives. She handed them to me and I asked, "Will we need spoons?"

She looked at Willa and asked, "Mommy, do we need spoons?"

Willa was placing a serving spoon in the large bowl of spaghetti and setting the bowl on the table. There wasn't much room for anything else. I put the knives and forks in their proper places and Willa handed me three teaspoons.

She grinned and said, "Have a seat and we'll eat."

I laughed and commented, "Poetry with every meal. That's a big deal."

Willa was laughing as she helped Peggy climb on top of a pillow to boost her high enough to eat at the table. I was still standing.

She pointed at the chair beside me and said, "Sit!"

I followed her command and we started dinner. Fortunately, Willa had thought of napkins. They were left over from one of Peggy's birthday parties and entirely appropriate. Those napkins made me feel much more comfortable. I was glad Willa didn't have fancy embroidered napkins, spaghetti sauce and linen napkins are incompatible.

We talked about many things as we ate. The spaghetti was really good, much better than anything I could have made. I began watching the level of light outdoors and Willa noticed my looks outside through the screen door.

"Do you have to be somewhere?" she asked.

"Oh, no. I don't like to drive at night. I think I'd better go soon, but I really don't want to. I'm enjoying this very much. You and Peggy have been great hosts." I pushed back the chair and started toward the door.

"You'll have to tell me about not wanting to drive at night. It was nice to have you over and I enjoyed it too. I'm sorry you have to go so soon."

"I hate to eat and run. I'm sorry. I'll tell you about it next week. Thanks for the great dinner."

Willa moved to the door and stood in the doorway forcing me to squeeze between her and the doorjamb. It was difficult to get past her without making body contact. I wanted to kiss her, but Peggy was watching. I knew Willa didn't want Peggy to see me kiss her mother. I couldn't help myself as I squeezed past her and my right hand slid over her breasts. I didn't consider it groping, but I didn't try to avoid touching her. Then I thought I had taken too much liberty contacting her sexy body.

"Good night, Willa, and thanks again." I hesitated outside the door and said, "Good night, Peggy."

As I walked to my car, Willa said, "I'm so happy you came over, Ned. We'll do it again—earlier in the day. See you Monday!" She waved goodbye and I waved back.

As I drove toward home in the twilight, I felt a little embarrassed that I had taken the freedom to give her a subtle squeeze as I exited her home. I'll have to apologize on Monday. I hope I didn't ruin our relationship. But Willa's parting words indicated she hadn't thought what had happened was going to impact our relationship negatively. I'll find out when she comes to work on Monday afternoon—if she shows up.

I had a visitor Monday when I was eating my lunch. I had closed my door and was looking over some email from university offices. The office where tests were printed had changed procedures to increase security, so in the future only professors could pick up printed exams. There was a knock on my door. I figured it was Willa showing up for work, but it was only 12:30. She usually spent the hour before work with Peggy.

"Come in." I looked away from my monitor toward the door as it opened. It was Lisa. I hadn't expected her, but her presence would certainly liven up lunch hour. She was wearing a short pink dress and a light-yellow sweater. As usual, she looked great. Those bright blue eyes always grabbed my attention. She looked like she was ready to ride on a float in an Easter parade.

"Come in, Lisa. Have a seat. Are you taking that thermodynamics class you wanted?"

I stood and moved toward her, but she took Willa's chair, looked up, and nodded.

"Uh-huh. I'm on my way to lecture. Dr. Addario is the professor. She changed the lecture time to 1:00 p.m., so I won't have to drive in the evening. I'm enjoying the class. I think I'm the only student that is shorter than she is. Most of the students are men." Lisa grinned and I smiled back.

"You are a tiny woman, Lisa, but you look great." I wanted to say how sexy she looked, but I refrained. I wasn't going to get into another relationship when I already had visions of a future with Willa.

"Thanks, Ned. Will you be able to come see me at the observatory?"

I wanted to say yes and we would arrange a time for my visit, but I couldn't get involved with two sexy women at the same time. I was afraid both relationships would fall apart. I would probably refer to one of these delectable creatures by the other's name and then all might be lost. My lack of experience with women would show up fast. Undoubtedly, both Lisa and Willa were far ahead of me when it came to relationships. The other thing that nagged at me was that they were both married. I wished if one of them were a divorcée, I would have an easy decision, but no such luck.

"I don't think I'll make it to the telescope until the semester is over. I have to finish my research or I won't receive tenure. All my free time has to be devoted to my project." I tried to look sorrowful, but I was lying. I hoped she couldn't tell. Any free time I had was to be devoted to Willa and Peggy. If that relationship fell apart, I would try to get together with Lisa. I hated to think of Lisa as a backup plan. She seemed so genuine and was very suggestive.

I was hoping Lisa would be leaving for class before Willa came for lab work, but that thought was lost a minute later. Willa came in from the hall, looked at Lisa and stepped back into the hallway.

I called out, "Come in, Willa. Go ahead and get started in the lab; I'll be with you in a few minutes." As Willa walked through my office, Lisa stood and picked up her notebook from my desk. We talked another minute or two standing in my office doorway before Lisa had to go to class on the second floor. We said goodbye and she headed for the elevator. My eyes followed her down the hall and when she made a motion to glance back at me, I ducked into my office.

Willa was watching me from the lab. "She likes you, Ned. She *really* likes you."

"I like her, too, but she's married. I'm only interested in one woman right now."

I watched Willa as she was weighing a sample. She didn't react to my comment.

"Peggy likes you. She said you were different from her daddy, but she still likes you."

I laughed. "Well, I like Peggy and her mother—a lot."

Willa smiled, but she still didn't look away from her work. I decided to apologize.

"I'm sorry I grabbed at you when I left. I shouldn't have done that, but at the time I wanted to hug and kiss you, but not in front of Peggy. She would get confused if her mom was kissing two men, one not her daddy—at least that was my thought."

"Hey, don't worry about it. I wanted you to do something. I didn't know if you were really attracted to me that way. That's why I forced you to squeeze past me at the door. I wanted to feel some body contact."

"I think you are very sexy, Willa. I don't understand why Steve doesn't treat you with great respect. You're smart, pretty, a great mom, and easy to talk to. Those are great qualities."

"Some of my friends told me not to marry him, but I have never followed friends' advice. I have to live my own life. I'm the one responsible for my mistakes. Maybe I made one—a big one." She raised her eyebrows and bit her lower lip. "But now I have Peggy. I'm so happy to have her."

I considered what she had said for a moment and responded, "I've made a few mistakes, too." I grinned, "More than a few. I was afraid to make mistakes in school. I couldn't handle it when people laughed at me. So, I withdrew—became an introvert. I found things I could do by myself."

"I don't think you're an introvert. You are a very good teacher. You communicate with others very well. All of your students I know like you." She smiled and paused for a second, looking away. "They don't like your tests though." She laughed and it was infectious. My eyes watered when I laughed. I wanted to hug her.

"I know my tests are difficult. I want to separate the good from the not-so-good. It's easier to assign grades that way. I don't want to give out an A grade for attendance; I want it to mean something. I'm glad you're a good student. When you were a youngster, I was a little afraid you would have problems with school, but here you are, an A student. I'm really proud of you."

Willa finished processing the chunk of meteorite as I unwrapped another sample that had recently arrived. It was the second sample from Mexico. There was a note in Spanish in the container, but I would have to ask one of my students to translate it for me or take it to the foreign language department. I'd try a student translation first. The note would go with me to my lectures on Wednesday.

Willa left for the children's center promptly at 2:00 p.m. Her parting words were, "Bye, Ned. See you tomorrow at 1:00 p.m."

Boy, she had a great smile. "Bye, Willa. Have a safe trip home."

The rest of the afternoon was spent going over departmental business with Beth and reviewing applications for graduate assistantships with the chemistry graduate coordinator, Dr. Thomas. I wasn't able to process any of the recently arrived meteorite samples, but I labelled and stored them before I went home for dinner.

During the week I decided to ask Willa if she and Peggy would like to have dinner with me Friday evening. I called Willa Wednesday night from home and she accepted. During our hour-long conversation, I told Willa I would pick them up at 4:30 Friday if that was okay. I asked if she liked seafood and she gave me a hearty yes. She and Peggy would be ready.

Although I would be driving home in the dark, I felt I knew the roads well enough to not have any problems. I had focused on a half-dozen landmarks when driving to Willa's home and back on the previous Saturday, so I wouldn't get lost. Also, I was used to stopping to ask for directions when in unfamiliar territory. That didn't bother me in the least. Besides, Willa probably was familiar with all the roads near her home; she could probably drive to the campus with her eyes closed. As soon as that last thought came to mind, I realized how lame it was.

Thursday at noon, I went home for lunch and called a seaside restaurant in Del Mar and made reservations. It wasn't a cheap place, but not too expensive either, but I didn't need to worry about money any longer; I had saved nearly $50,000 in almost six years.

CHAPTER 19

FRIDAY EVENING was great. I told Willa money was not a problem; order anything she desired. We watched the boats in the harbor moving around like amoebae in a Petri dish. About half the vessels had sails, and as we got ready to order, there was a spectacular sunset splashing red, orange, and yellow hues across the beach and buildings.

"Peggy! Look at everything! It's almost like the coastline is on fire!" Willa's excitement inhabited us as we watched the sun sink into the ocean water horizon.

Peggy said she didn't want fish so Willa ordered her the children's spaghetti dinner. We could tell Peggy enjoyed her dinner by the amount of sauce that decorated her face and fingers, she hadn't yet mastered a fork. A Hollywood makeup artist couldn't have done a better job. The waitress brought us a small damp towel for Peggy's clean up. I left the server a generous tip.

Willa helped me with directions and we arrived at her home a few minutes after eight o'clock. Peggy had fallen asleep in the car and I carried her to her bedroom. I was beginning to enjoy being a substitute father for Peggy. I stepped out to the living room while Willa got Peg ready for bed. When Willa came from Peggy's bedroom, we sat on the sofa and talked for about ten minutes.

"I've got to go, Willa. I'm going to have to take my time returning home. I can't drive well at night—oncoming headlights make it very difficult to see, so I drive slowly. I'm glad you and Peggy joined me for dinner. I really enjoyed your company."

"Thank you, Ned. I had a wonderful time. I was happy to share that beautiful sunset with you. I'll see you again on Monday. I'm going to spend the weekend cleaning, doing laundry, and studying for your class and calculus. Tests will be coming up before long." She smiled at me as a hint of encouragement to divulge what I had planned for the exam.

"Very clever, sweetie, but I'm not going to fall for that."

She looked surprised. "Oh! I don't expect you to give me any tips different from what you would tell the class. I'm surprised you would think that of me." She looked very serious.

"I'm sorry—I thought you were trying to sneak some information."

She gave a little laugh and said, "I wanted to see what you would do, Ned. You didn't fall for it. That's another thing I like about you—your honesty."

I slid closer to Willa, put my hand around her neck and kissed her. She didn't try to avoid the touch of our lips and without moving away, she placed her hand on my cheek and returned the kiss.

We held hands in silence. I didn't want to move away from her warm inviting body, but I had to hit the road. I didn't think I should try to stay the night; I didn't even want to suggest it. I imagined Willa was thinking about her relationship with Steve.

I grinned, "I'm getting very warm. I'd better go. I'll put the windows down and cool off on the way home." I got up and she followed me to the door. "Good night, Willa. See you Monday."

"Night, Ned. Be careful on your way home."

As I got in my car, I watched Willa close the front door. When the porch light was extinguished, I started the engine and began the stressful trip home in the dark. I watched for landmarks and followed my normal route back to Ocean Vista. Driving in town was a relief; the streets to my apartment were well-known and had bright lights. I parked and went inside, tuned in the late TV news, watched it for about ten minutes and went to bed—but not to sleep. All I could think about was Willa—she appeared to have the same feelings for me as I did for her. Was she going to divorce Steve? I finally drifted off to sleep around 2:00 a.m.

My mind was permeated with thoughts of Willa and Peggy the entire weekend, but I forced myself to begin the analysis of the iron isotope ratios of the meteorite fragments. After tabulating only twenty-five samples, I could see there was a slight trend forming. But I had over 150 samples to go and that trend might disappear with a larger population. I still hoped that I would be able to see an association of a meteorite with its radiant and therefore assign a known source to fragments that had no recorded radiant.

Much more had to be done in the next thirteen weeks. I didn't have much leeway with time: finish the samples, analyze the data, write a paper, and submit it for publication. I felt like a mountaineer without any other aids but bare fingers and climbing boots. If it weren't for an able assistant, I would have to give up. Perhaps I wasn't meant to stay at Ocean Vista.

Without a publication in six years, what university would hire me? I would have to find a job in industry, at a community college, or at a high school. My future was looking dismal. As long as I was still breathing, I would attempt to finish my project, do an admirable teaching job, and assist in finding a new geology faculty member, preferably someone at the associate professor level to replace Dr. Reynolds. I doubted whether the administration would be willing to hire a full professor; it would be too costly. Unfortunately, restrictive budgets often determine the quality of teachers at small universities.

I stayed home Sunday evening and prepared a week's lectures, concentrating on stratigraphy. The students were starting to feel more comfortable with the methods I was using in my lectures. I started thinking of the lectures as discussions—nearly half the class time was being taken up with contributions by the students. I was becoming a much better listener, cutting down on lecture time, which was a bit strange for me. I was beginning to see where the misunderstandings and misconceptions were originating. I might be able to squeeze out a lesser paper for a teaching journal, saving me as a faculty member. I began to question whether I wanted to remain in Southern California.

As I brushed my teeth, it suddenly occurred to me that the Dean of the College of Arts and Sciences was the only administrator I had to impress. I no longer had a chairman to worry about. I read from one of my texts—the one for Willa's class, before I went to sleep. As I closed the text and turned out my reading light, I did something I had never done before; I said a prayer for Willa and Peggy. I wanted them to be safe and happy, even if I wouldn't be in their lives.

The last time I remembered saying a prayer was when I was fourteen years old. I had prayed that my eyes would not get worse, because that would require Mom and Dad having to pay for cataract operations. My family was not well off, and I had made no promises to God. My eyes got slightly worse during high school, but I was able to see well enough to go to college, work when absolutely necessary to support my education, and finish my Ph.D. over a period of eighteen years. Driving at night was a major problem, but one I could handle if I knew the roads well enough. I thought I had conquered that difficulty by adequate preparation.

Willa and I made good progress on my research the next week. With both of us processing samples, we finished all the specimens that had been submitted, a total of 173.

Willa invited me over on Saturday and we took Peggy to the beach. I thought it was a bit too cold for swimming, but Willa put on her one-piece and swam for a few minutes while I watched Peggy. I was such a poor swimmer, I never ventured into ocean water deeper than my knees. Peggy and I found some interesting shells and some colorful pebbles. Willa looked fantastic in her purple swimsuit.

We ate lunch Willa had prepared and listened to music from my battery-operated transistor radio. After two hours on the beach, Willa said she had to shower to get the sea water washed from her hair, so we drove back to her house. We had been on the sand and in the water for three enjoyable hours.

The activity on the beach making sandcastles plus walking in the sand picking up shells and colored rocks had worn Peggy out. Willa put her to bed for a nap and then took a shower. I took off my shoes to shake out sand and was leaning back on the sofa with my stocking feet on the cushions when Willa came into the living room wrapped in a beach towel. I started to swing my legs down to make room for her, but she said, "No, stay the way you are."

As Willa walked slowly toward me with her arms extended to the side, the towel slowly unwound and dropped to the floor. She stood next to me completely naked—absolutely beautiful. I circled her legs with my left arm and pulled her closer.

She smiled and said, "Let me help you with your clothes." She loosened my belt and unzipped my pants before I had much of a chance to react; my eyes were focused on her voluptuous body.

We made love on the sofa until we were both out of breath. She let her body sink onto mine and we rested in each other's arms.

"Are you all right doing this?" I asked.

She didn't answer at first, just smiled and kissed me for a long time. "I've been thinking about this for some time. When Steve travels to other ports I know he screws around with other women. Word gets back to me from his friends' wives. If he's going to do that, then I have no reason to abstain while he's gone. Besides, I think you are wonderful."

I thanked her and kissed her again. "I'm afraid I'm a novice at making love, Willa."

"You taught me to read. I'll teach you what I can about having sex. It should be easy for you. You were ready for action today."

"When I saw you naked, I thought I was going to explode. I knew I was going to have trouble getting my undershorts off. An obstruction was in the way." I grinned.

She was stroking me very delicately. I was concerned about not using a condom and mentioned that to her.

"Don't worry about it; I had a tubal ligation after giving birth to Peggy. I can't get pregnant. It makes things easier and more enjoyable for me; no worries."

"Me, too." My erection was growing again and she said, "Repeat performance?"

I nodded and she straddled my legs again. Our coupling lasted much longer the second time. We paced ourselves to prolong the enjoyment, and afterwards, we took a shower together.

We took turns soaping each other's bodies. My hands lingered over her soft, beautifully sculptured breasts covered in suds. We would have run out of hot water before I got tired of touching her body. As the water began to cool, we stepped out of the shower, dried off, and assisted each other getting dressed. I had never enjoyed an afternoon like that in my entire life.

I was going to have a major problem lecturing with Willa sitting in class. I would have to keep from looking at her. I wondered what would happen if another student found out about us.

The remainder of the spring semester was deluged with research activities and Willa. I was happy to see the research winding down, but I couldn't get enough of Willa. We met every Saturday at her house or my apartment. We went out a few times, but always away from the campus and far from San Diego to avoid any sightings by acquaintances. Even then, I could not exhibit any affection when out in public. I once made the mistake of putting my hand around her waist. She scowled at me and promptly swatted away my hand. I felt about as small as I ever had in my entire life; holding her that way had seemed so natural. I began to think that my love for her was not reciprocal.

After one of our love-making activities, Willa asked, "What will you do when Steve comes back, Ned?"

I knew then that I was on a dead-end street. I thought about it briefly and answered, "It will take me a few weeks to get over it, but I'll live." That had been a lie. I was madly in love with Willa. I will never forget her or the times we had together and with Peggy. I wanted Willa to get a divorce, we would marry, and I would adopt Peggy, but after that exchange, I knew our time together was soon to arrive at an unhappy conclusion, at least in my case. I didn't want our relationship to change or end. I didn't know how she felt and was afraid to ask.

The day after the semester ended I received a call at home Monday evening. It was Willa.

"Steve's coming back Wednesday so we won't be able to see each other anymore."

That was all she said. I didn't know what to say in return except to acknowledge what she had said. I had a lump in my throat, but I was able to say, "I understand. I'm going to miss you, Willa. Are you going to come by my office to say goodbye?"

"Yes, I promise. I have some things to pick up—some final exams and a notebook. I'll see you in a few days. Bye."

"Bye, Willa." I had heard no indication of any sorrow or regret in her voice, just a statement of fact. The click of the telephone disconnecting seemed very loud, almost like a door slamming shut. I sat by the phone for several minutes thinking that I should never have let our relationship go as far as it did. But I wanted to see Willa at least one more time to say a real goodbye. I knew I would shed some tears. I almost regretted the thought of seeing her one last time, but I wanted to find out what her plans were. From the way she had talked, I had to assume we would never see each other again.

A week passed and there was still no sign of Willa. I couldn't have missed her, I was in my office continuously, except for breakfast, dinner, and sleeping. I spent many hours finishing up my research paper. I had determined there was only one radiant that differed in iron isotopes compared with all the others. Leonid meteorites exhibited a different isotopic distribution than all the other sources, suggesting the iron was from another source, perhaps some debris captured by the sun during a close approach of another star in the early days of the formation of the Milky Way. I was also able to send off a brief paper to *The Journal of Geologic Education.*

After eleven days of waiting, I decided to drive to Willa's and talk to her. I took some test papers and her lab notebook with me. It was Friday afternoon about 2:00 p.m. when I arrived at her Del Mar address. I went to the door and Willa stepped out on the porch.

"What are you doing here? You have to go. You can't be here." She hardly looked at me.

I gave her the notebook and papers and started toward my car. I looked back and she had gone in the house and slammed the door. I started the car and drove away, but not very far before tears had pooled on my glasses and my vision was being obstructed. The road was blurring, so I pulled over to the shoulder and broke down weeping like a child that has lost a parent. It took several minutes to quell the sobbing enough to drive. I cried all the way back to my apartment. Driving was difficult, but

I made the journey home without incident. I sat on the sofa and cried some more until there were no more tears.

During the following weeks, whenever I came upon something Willa had touched, I threw it in the trash, except the data she had collected for me. I had to save that for my publication. I felt like removing her name from the acknowledgements in my article, but I couldn't be that mean. She deserved some recognition for the work she had done.

Fortunately, both papers were accepted and I received tenure that summer. Due to the emotional toll I suffered, I had difficulty controlling my blood glucose levels and started walking and jogging to assist the insulin. During the jogging exercises, I began to think of having cataract surgery to clear my vision; I had put up with poor eyesight long enough. The night driving difficulty had to be put in the past if possible. Surgery on my left eye was done first and the next summer, my right eye was cleared. As it turned out, I still didn't like to drive at night, although after surgery, I didn't have to worry any longer about driving off the roadway in the dark. The lights from on-coming vehicles no longer blinded me, but I never did like to drive at night. After surgery, I was amazed that I could actually see individual leaves on trees, whereas before, the foliage was just a green blob.

About a year after Willa had left school, I received a letter from her, but the return address was illegible. I almost didn't open the envelope, but I waited until nearly everyone had left the building before I looked inside. I didn't want anyone to see me red-eyed. It was a greeting card asking me to be her valentine. I sat and wondered about that card for some time. I felt I had been used as a temporary replacement for her husband and then discarded. Since there was no return address, I deposited the card and envelope in the trash. I had been deeply hurt by her; I felt she had just cast me aside.

About six months later, Willa called me to ask if I would give her a recommendation and after we talked for a short period, I agreed to give her a very strong evaluation. She didn't volunteer anything about Peggy and I didn't ask. She said nothing about the valentine; neither did I. I wished her good luck in her search for a job.

A week after talking to Willa, I received a call from a potential employer and I gave her a great recommendation. Despite what had happened, I still loved Willa and wanted her to have a good job and future. I had no doubts that she would soon be remarried.

I never saw Lisa again. My devotion to Willa was so consuming, I never even had thoughts of hooking up with her after September and I had become intimate. Years after September had gone and upon occasion she entered my mind briefly, I had thoughts of Lisa, too, and whether I should have pursued her rather than Willa. Perhaps she had met someone in her physics class; she had never returned to my office during that semester or later. Maybe she had discovered I was interested in Willa. I hoped she was having a fruitful and happy life. I used to wonder if I could have used a time machine and been able to have a do-over, would I have hooked up with Lisa—who knows?

CHAPTER 20

FOR THE next year or so, I continued prayers for Willa and Peggy because it was the right thing to do. I truly wished them the best. I had suffered emotionally but I finally realized the wisdom of one of the Commandments. But as time passed, the deep wounds began to fade and the prayers were discontinued. What had occurred had to have been the best for all. I don't remember making a conscious decision to stop the entreaties, I guess I just began to forget that nighttime practice.

Three years later, around five years since Willa had gone, I met a young German woman. She was a graduate student in the communications department and we hit it off. Katharina Klepper was a nice looking woman, but she was about forty pounds overweight. She had a wonderful smile and possessed an intriguing sense of humor. After completing her communications degree, she worked at two different radio stations in San Diego so we were able to see each other quite often as friends. Coffee was our drink of choice at McDonalds.

We had known each other for about two years when she surprised me by moving in; we hadn't discussed the matter, but I didn't object. A couple of years after having eye surgery I had moved from my old apartment to a house farther from campus where my neighbors were not partiers into early morning hours.

Kathy had gone on a diet and lost a lot of weight, although her face remained pleasantly round. When in San Diego, she had joined a gym and became a very nice looking woman. Six months after she moved in with me, we were married and she quit her radio station jobs to attend business school, but she had to commute to San Diego to attend the classes she wanted. She arranged to have all afternoon sessions.

We tried to have a baby, but I think my swimmers were damaged when I had mumps at the age of twenty-three. That was a painful three-week ordeal when I was a young man. We suffered a miscarriage and I believe that led to Kathy wanting a divorce. She was very competitive with a good friend of hers who had given birth to a healthy baby. I was so busy at the university I didn't look into the matter by consulting the medical community. We could have tried again.

I later discovered miscarriages are not uncommon, but we were both ignorant of the facts, or it could have been Kathy just wanted out. She moved to Florida after nearly three years of marriage. I was both happy and sad to see her drive away. I couldn't understand my ambivalent feelings.

After that fiasco, I pretty much gave up on women. I think I am too easily deceived by the opposite sex. Breakups drained me emotionally and I decided I'd rather be alone than with someone that treated me as a throw-away. I didn't have my eyes closed, however, and there were several young women that I was attracted to, but they had no intention of a meaningful relationship. They were just brown-nosing students. Besides, they were too young for me, less than half my age.

As the years passed, twenty-two at Ocean Vista, I began to lose interest in teaching. It wasn't enjoyable any longer. Most of my good friends were retiring, leaving the area, and returning to their home states. Two years later, in 2006, I decided to retire and move to the Pacific Northwest. The forests, rivers, lakes, and majestic Mt. Hood looked very inviting in photos of Oregon on the Internet. After a year of renting, I bought a split-level fixer-upper near Portland, Oregon. I have always been good with tools and I like woodworking. My retirement home was near a picturesque creek. I began renovations by ripping out the old carpets, molding, and the entire floor in the kitchen.

That floor had to go. I removed a layer of vinyl tile and three layers of linoleum that had seen better days—much better days. As I worked on the kitchen, I used the downstairs family room as a mess hall. A refrigerator, a microwave, and an old card table made a temporary kitchenette. Paper plates and plastic utensils were cheap and didn't require washing. They were ideal.

It took nearly three months before I had the upstairs kitchen completely rebuilt. There were other projects throughout the house that needed attention, too. I made a list of things to do and it was overwhelming. I had to prioritize.

Not long after redoing the kitchen, I realized I needed a shop for my major tools: table saw, router, compound miter saw, shaper, and drill press. I had to get a concrete pad poured and then obtain a permit from the city for the structure, a twelve by sixteen foot building no higher than ten feet because of the close neighbors—regulations to follow.

Sometimes I ran out of energy and took time off from renovating, but what was I to do? I needed a hobby that didn't require a large investment of funds. My finances were not unlimited, but I began making large payments on my mortgage. I was using up my savings, but paying off the mortgage at a rapid rate, saving money in the long haul.

I have always liked walking as a form of exercise: little impact on joints, no problems breathing, nice talks with neighbors, fresh air, and squirrels and birds to watch. Of course there was one slight drawback: barking dogs, but I gradually made friends with most of them. I carried doggy treats most of the time.

As I was walking one day, I thought of an idea for a story. That was the spark that ignited my writing career. New adventure stories were popping into my head almost every time I walked. As I began to enjoy writing, the time spent on renovations decreased dramatically. Many of my remodeling projects remained unfinished for many months as writing absorbed the majority of my waking hours.

Invariably, researching new ideas led to Internet searches of various kinds. Not long after I had begun writing, I searched for Willa, but I didn't know where she lived. I entered her name from the old class lists and found a dozen Septembers of about her age. Gradual elimination because of race, birthdate, and size of family led me to a photo of Willa. I guessed the picture to be fairly recent. She was as beautiful as ever. She still looked as she did many years earlier.

She had remarried, as I expected. That was in 2014; she would have been fifty years old then, eight years after I had retired. I had no clue how to contact her, so I ended the search. I was pleased that she had a good life, at least I hoped so. I wanted to ask Willa how Peggy was and find out if Willa was a grandmother yet. I had loved little Peggy, too. I hoped she had married into a good family.

About every six to eight months or so, I would see if I could contact Willa. One day I saw an email address that might be hers. I emailed and asked if it was the September I had known. I didn't get an answer, but the email wasn't rejected as undelivered. A year or so later, I sent a birthday greeting and said I didn't expect a reply. I didn't want her to think I was trying to get back together, I just wanted to see what she was doing—find out if she was healthy and still working. Again, I got no answer. I wondered, as I had many times before, if our relationship had always been a sham. I finally concluded that she had never loved me. I had suffered a snow job. No, it had been a real blizzard.

Late one night I took a break from working on my tenth book; I had begun writing novels after retiring. I had reached an impasse that I had to overcome. I saved the unfinished document and started to the kitchen to get some decaf and a cookie. I didn't want to be kept from sleep until the early morning hours because of the dreaded caffeine in regular brew. I turned on the TV as I walked past it on the way to the kitchen. I wanted to catch the late local news.

I had the volume turned up; I had lost the hearing on my left side from a bout with a virus and hearing on my right side wasn't especially good. When I explained my poor hearing to others, I always had to laugh. Now, when I mow the lawn, I wear an earplug—one in my right ear. As I poured the coffee, prepared earlier, and put it in the microwave to warm up, I heard the newscaster say a woman had been discovered alone on a mountain road and she had been transported to the Portland NE Hospital. She was unconscious when found, had no ID, and was now in a drug induced coma. Jane Doe had suffered a severe head injury.

When I saw a photo of the woman lying in a hospital bed and attached to a respirator, I gasped, "Jesus, I think that's Willa!" What could have happened and why would she be in the mountains of

Oregon? It was 11:18 p.m., too late to call the hospital. They would probably give me the runaround at this late hour. I decided to drive to the hospital in the morning and see if I could get into the intensive care unit. I began preparing myself for an array of questions that I might be asked when I got there. As I was thinking of possible questions, I felt like I was readying to be a defense witness at a murder trial.

I didn't sleep well and got up early, took a shower, and dressed while eating my usual breakfast. I was ready to set out for the hospital at 7:30 a.m. but I sat down, tried to relax, and drank another cup of decaf; I didn't want to arrive at the hospital too early. Previous experiences with hospital personnel at the front desk early in the morning led me to anticipate somewhat surly attitudes as if I were visiting a prisoner at the state penitentiary.

All I could think of was that picture I saw of Willa with her head bandaged and tubes in her mouth and nose. I left for the hospital at 8:00. It would take me a little over thirty minutes on Glisan Street if I didn't exceed the speed limit. I had to grin as I travelled west down Glisan. Glisan was pronounced Gleason, as in Jackie Gleason, the entertainer. It must have been a family name, and they pronounced Glisan as Gleason.

Traffic was a mess as I approached the hospital complex. Everyone was trying to get to work at the same time or had early morning appointments. The red lights were no help. I entered the parking garage and found a spot on the top floor after circling around and around. It was 8:50 when I locked my car and started walking to the main desk. Surely, all hospital personnel would be awake and in good spirits by now.

Inside the main entrance, I saw the information desk. As I homed in on her position, the attendant smiled and asked, "May I help you?"

"I hope so. I saw a picture on the news last night of a woman in a coma. I'm pretty sure I know her."

"Oh, that's very good news. The ICU nurse will want to talk to you. Please go to the fifth floor, I'll tell them you're coming up. What's your name?"

"Dr. Ned Curtis."

"Oh! You're a physician?"

"No. PhD in Geology. I believe the comatose woman in the news was one of my students long ago. I lost track of her."

"Nurse Landis will speak to you upstairs. Take elevator A. Press button five."

"Thank you, nurse Jenkins." I had noticed the embroidered name on her uniform. She smiled.

I had an uncomfortable feeling as I rode the elevator. I had never spent much time in a hospital and I was a little nervous in the unfamiliar surroundings. But I think most of the nerves were from the unexpected reaction that awaited when I saw Willa. I wondered what the nurse would ask me and what the prognosis was for Willa. I said a little prayer for her just before the elevator stopped, a buzzer sounded, and the door slid open.

The hallway curved to the left where an enclosure of workstations monitored the various patients' vital signs.

"Are you Dr. Curtis?" It was an administrative person dressed in a blue uniform as opposed to the nurses' light pastel-pink ones. She had her hair pulled back in a bun and wore large plastic framed glasses. She looked very official as if she worked in the financial office.

"Yes, ma'am."

"Please follow me."

I did—into an office with meager furnishings. She shut the door, motioned for me to take a seat and said, "I'm Lynette Landis. I interview visitors to patients in the ICU."

We shook hands and I said, "September was a student of mine about thirty years ago. I was shocked to see her photo on the local news last night."

"You are sure she is a former student of yours? Thirty years is a long time; faces change over time."

"Pretty sure. If you want to check, she has a cesarean scar and a small mole on her right hip."

Nurse Landis pursed her lips, thought for a moment, and replied, "I won't ask how you know that." I could tell she had already determined how I knew that. I didn't care. She could think anything she wanted. I was there to see if I could help Willa.

"What is her full name?"

"When I knew her it was September Howard. She was married to Steven Howard, who was in the Navy, and they had a daughter named Peggy. They were headed toward a divorce in 1988. I lost track of them. I assume she remarried, but I don't know her married name. Will that help you find out her full name?"

"Do you know where she lived?"

"When she was a young girl, about eight or nine, she lived in Delight, Texas. Her mother worked in Waco. Her mother's name was Helen Walker. Oh! Her dad was killed in an accident when she was about ten."

Nurse Landis sighed, "Some people have a tough life, don't they?" She put down her pad and pen and asked, "Do you want to see September?"

I stood and said, "I sure do. The news said she's in a coma. Is there anything I can do for her?"

"Maybe. Follow me and we'll visit her. Don't be shocked by the condition she's in. She has some facial bruising and her skull is bandaged. She was initially in room 412, but we moved her to the ICU. The doctors had to relieve pressure by boring some small holes in her skull. They'll heal over when she recovers. But remember, she won't know you're here. She's in a drug-induced coma now."

We moved a short distance down a corridor and passed through two sets of locked doors. The isolation rooms were slightly pressurized to keep foreign particles in the ICU to a minimum. As we passed through the second set of doors, a middle aged man and a golden retriever were exiting. I stepped to the side, frowned, and looked at the nurse.

"That's a therapy dog and her handler. The dog's name is Honey and the trainer is Vaughn Wilson. We call him VW." She smiled and continued, "Gravely ill patients sometimes respond favorably to an animal."

CHAPTER 21

ANOTHER NURSE joined Mrs. Landis and me. I shook hands with Trish Johnson and we walked to the last of the four rooms along the east wall. Each room had a bed and an assortment of equipment including monitors and wall valves for gases. The rooms were not spacious; there was only a foldup chair for a single visitor. I could see Willa's oxygen unit was attached to a nasal cannula after the gas had been bubbled through an aqueous solution to add water vapor to the dry gas.

Willa hadn't changed much in the last thirty years; she appeared to be sleeping peacefully. Her skin looked very normal—no pale tones were evident, but her face had a purplish bruise on the left side from her ear lobe to above her eyebrow. Her hair had apparently been shaved from her skull, and the dome of her head was bandaged. According to the nurses, she didn't have any broken bones.

Trish stood beside me and commented, "Nothing was broken, but she hit her head on something very hard or with violent force; maybe both. We've been monitoring her vitals closely. She seems to be holding her own, but we're worried about a stroke occurring.

I noticed her fingers moving but not in any regular manner. Not like she was typing or anything like that—just a slight movement of her index fingers. I pointed to her fingers and Trish said, "That's common; it's not a conscious thing." I was disappointed, hoping for a sign of conscious effort. Willa had always been so strong physically and mentally; I hated to see her this way. I had never seen her this vulnerable before.

"We started weaning her from the drugs last night. She might begin to respond to voices before long. Maybe this afternoon. Would you like to sit with her for a bit?"

I couldn't get my mouth open to speak, but I nodded. I could feel tears welling up and I was afraid my voice would crack, so I didn't say anything. That's when I knew I still loved Willa.

I'd sit with her as long as it took. She would come to or pass on before I left her at the hospital alone. I would be with her no matter what.

Trish brought me a padded chair from another room and I sat beside the bed holding Willa's left hand in both of mine. It was warm and I could feel an occasional finger movement. Willa was still as beautiful as she was many years ago. There were a few tiny lines about her eyes, but they were the only changes I noticed. She had never needed much makeup; her eye lashes and eyebrows were still full and delicately shaped—perfect for her attractive face.

I prayed that she would awaken and see me sitting beside her and know I had never forgotten our times together years ago. I had been there about an hour when Trish returned to check on Willa. The nurse's station was constantly monitoring her vital signs, but depending on the patient, periodic visits were carried out following a definite schedule.

"Mr. Curtis, would you like to go for coffee or a snack? There is a snack bar two floors below. They have fruit, coffee, tea, sweet rolls, and a few other things you might enjoy. There are also public bathrooms available."

"Thank you—that's a good idea. I'll take a break and come back in half-an-hour."

"You'd better make that about an hour. We have to change sheets and adjust the patient's position. We don't want any bed sores to develop."

"Okay. I'll be back." I checked my watch for the time.

I knew the fluids flowing into Willa's arm were being watched and adjusted periodically and she must have a catheter, although I hadn't noticed one. It was probably concealed by the bedcovers. I took the stairs at the end of the hallway and descended two floors. It felt good to exercise my leg muscles. I had been sitting too long, nearly fifty-five minutes; riding in the car and sitting in the ICU had consumed equivalent amounts of time. The little commissary was stocked with self-serve machines, condiments, and three small tables capable of seating about a dozen staff and visitors. There was a note board on the wall that said there was a public cafeteria in the basement where a much larger selection of food was available.

I checked my blood glucose and decided to have half a tuna sandwich and coffee. The sandwich was a dollar and the coffee was free. I sat at one of the tables and liberated the sandwich from its tightly wrapped plastic covering with some difficulty; I could have used a pair of scissors. The tuna fish was cold, as were my fingers, but the coffee warmed my stomach and hands. I should have chosen ham and egg instead of tuna and warmed it in the microwave.

I sipped the coffee and thought of Willa in that hospital bed fighting to stay alive. I knew she was a physically strong woman and I hoped she had the will to recover. I had to know why she was in Oregon and in the mountains by herself. I wondered if Peggy knew where her mother was. I got another cup of coffee and looked out the window at the traffic on Interstate 84 wondering where all those people were going. I planned on returning to Willa's side at 10:30. My watch read 10:12; eighteen minutes remained before I climbed back up two flights of metal and concrete stairs. I said another prayer for Willa and closed my eyes for a few minutes.

At 10:27 I started back to the ICU complex. When I reached the fourth floor landing, Trish was coming down the stairs from the fifth floor with another nurse I didn't recognize.

"Mr. Curtis. You can sit with your friend now. Vaughn and Honey are with her. Don't be surprised—but they usually stay for only fifteen minutes."

I frowned at first, but then I remembered Honey was the therapy dog and Vaughn was her handler. I gave a little smile, "Thanks for the warning."

September stepped out on the porch and watched for the SUV to park in front of the garage, but the car wasn't there. She couldn't hear any car sounds, no tires crunching on gravel, no engine noises, no squeak of brakes, no doors shutting, nothing but the soughing of wind in the trees. Where were Von and Honey? She started around the cabin, stopped at each corner and listened, then moved on until she had circled the structure. There was no sign of the car. What had she seen from the window? Had she imagined seeing the SUV because she wanted so much for Von and Honey to be back?

She began to feel chilly so she returned to the living room and wrapped the afghan from the sofa around her shoulders and moved about to peer out all the windows. Had she hallucinated? She sat on the sofa and thought, where is Von? He should be back by now. Could he be playing a trick on me? That was it! He'll be knocking on the door any time now. But she wasn't going to let him in right away. She'd sit and listen for him to ask her to open the door. He'd have to say please before she'd let him in.

September sat there for a time before she got up and went to the kitchen to make tea. She nibbled on a cookie while waiting for the water to boil and occasionally looked out the kitchen window. Right after she sat at the kitchen table and took a sip of tea, she heard voices and a scratching at the front door. Was it Revo and Rover, or was it Von and Honey? Her mind was set; she wasn't going to run to the door. She'd wait until she heard a voice she recognized. But she heard unfamiliar women's voices; why would women be outside the cabin? She'd better take a look.

With the afghan draped over her shoulders, she slipped on her fuzzy blue bedroom slippers and walked quickly to the front door. At first glance, she saw nothing from the peephole; no one was there, but then her eyes caught some movement toward the bottom of the door. A dog's tail was swishing back and forth. It must be Honey!

September unlocked the door, swung it wide and there, looking up at her, was Honey, waiting patiently to be let into the cabin. She couldn't understand how Honey got to the cabin without Von.

"Honey! Come in! Where is Von?"

Honey dashed between September's legs and headed for the kitchen to find her food and water. September stepped out on the porch and looked around, but she saw nothing had changed. Von wasn't there. Where was their car? No women were present either but she heard female voices. She went back inside, locked the door, and followed Honey's trail into the kitchen.

September knelt beside Honey and began to pet her. "Where have you been, Honey? I've missed you so much." Honey looked up at September and then moved slightly to drink water from the bowl adjacent to her food. September stood and heard voices again. A woman's voice first and then a man's. He was saying "Willa." Only two men ever called her Willa: her daddy and Ned, her college teacher and lover, but her father passed away years ago. Could the voice she was hearing be Ned's? It doesn't sound like Von; Von's voice isn't as soothing and as pleasant as Ned's.

She could tell the voices were coming from outside the house, but she had looked before and no one was there; surely they wouldn't be on the roof or concealed by the trees. Ned couldn't know she was in the mountains of Oregon with Von and Honey. How would he have known to come to the cabin?

I watched Willa as Honey, the therapy dog, nestled against Willa's leg. Surprising to all of us, Willa's fingers began to move and her hand lifted from the bed to rest on Honey's shoulders. She began caressing the dog.

Trish exclaimed, "Look! She's moving her hand and arm on the dog! She's petting Honey!"

I touched Willa's hand with mine and said, "Willa, this is Ned. I'm here with you. Can you open your eyes?"

Ned's words didn't make any sense to Willa; she had her eyes open; she was petting Honey and turning her head to listen to the voices from the front of the house. She stood, frowning, and began walking toward the front door. She spoke out, "Ned? Is that you? I hear your voice but I can't see you. I'm looking outside, but no one is there. Where are you?"

"Willa, you are in a hospital bed. You were injured. Your eyes are closed—you can't see anything real. What you are seeing is in your imagination. You must open your eyes. I want you to see me. Please— open your eyes."

Trish put her hand on my shoulder and said, "Mr. Curtis. Tell her we will shine a light in her eyes. I will help her open them."

"Okay." I turned to Willa, "Willa, a nurse will help you open your eyes. She is going to shine a light on your eyelids. You should see a flash of light—like car lights shining across a window shade in a house. Then open your eyes."

I looked at Trish, she nodded and said, "Okay, September, here comes the light."

We watched as Willa's eyelids began flickering, opening just a crack. Trish used her light again and Willa's eyelids parted significantly. Then she squinted as if sunlight was too bright and closed her eyes again—but just for a second. She suddenly opened her eyes wide and looked directly at me.

"Ned! It's you. Oh, I've found you!" She reached toward me and I grasped her hand. Trish stepped closer to the bed and put her hand on Willa's shoulder.

Trish glanced at me, "I don't want her to move suddenly; she's got to take it easy. It will probably be several days before she is out of trouble. I've sent for Dr. Trumbliss. She'll want to examine September. I'm sure the doctor wants her to be quiet for a while."

"I understand. How long can I stay?"

"About a-half-hour, Mr. Curtis. I think that should be a safe period of time. I'll let you talk for a few minutes. Let's get Honey off the bed. I think she's accomplished her goal."

Vaughn scooped up the dog, put her on the floor and they left the room.

I had Willa's left hand sandwiched between my palms. She grabbed some of my fingers and squeezed.

"Hey, not so hard. You want to put me in the hospital?"

Willa smiled, lessened her grip, and said, "Just making sure I'm not dreaming. I had the strangest dream about being in a mountain cabin. My husband, Von, and our dog, Honey, left me all alone."

I smiled and commented, "The therapy dog's name is Honey and the handler's name is Vaughn. They just left to see other patients. What is your present husband's name?"

Willa shook her head. "It was Mark Hilliard. He passed away three years ago. I haven't remarried."

"How is Peggy?"

"Oh, you remember her! She's just fine. She married a really nice guy and they have two little boys, Ben and George. Ben is five and George is two. They keep Peg pretty busy—she's a stay-at-home mom."

"And what does her husband do?

She smiled, "He's a college professor, like you, at Baylor. He teaches history."

"You live in Waco now?"

"I did until about a month ago. I sold my house and bought a nice car." She gave me a puzzled look. "Do you know where my car is?"

I shook my head. "That's how you got to Oregon? You drove from Waco?"

Willa smiled and nodded. "It was a long drive to California and then up the coast to Oregon. It's so beautiful here—I'm glad I came."

"All I know is that you were found in the snow beside a mountain road. Nobody saw a car. The police couldn't figure out who you were, so they asked the TV stations to broadcast your picture. I saw it and came to the hospital this morning."

Willa gave me a quizzical look. "Someone took my car?"

"We don't know. Do you remember going off the road in the snow?"

She was silent, apparently trying to think of what had happened. She stared ahead and then replied, "I don't remember. I was driving on a mountain road—I think I made a wrong turn, but I kept going; looking for a sign so I could figure out where I was. I didn't get the Global Positioning System in my car. I must have gone off the road, but where is my car?"

"Don't worry, I'll ask the police about it. Maybe somebody has found it. Do you remember the license number?"

She thought for a few seconds and said, "No, but it has Texas plates. I bought it in Waco. It's a white Subaru Forester. The license number is in my purse; look in there."

"Mr. Curtis?"

It was Trish, the nurse. She said what I expected. My time to visit with Willa was up for the day.

"You may come back and spend more time with September tomorrow if you like."

I squeezed Willa's hand and said, "Bye, Willa. I'll be back in the morning. Get some rest."

CHAPTER 22

BEFORE I could release her hand, she pulled me closer and said, "I have something I have to tell you. You're coming back, aren't you?"

I smiled and lifted her hand to my lips. I kissed her fingers and said, "Don't you worry about that. I'll be here as soon as they'll let me in." I backed out of the ICU waving to September. As I rode the elevator to the first floor, an image of eight-year-old Willa infiltrated my thoughts; I remembered her falling down in the front yard of my rental years ago. I wanted to help her overcome the problems she was having, but this time it had nothing to do with reading. This time it involved something much more important: staying alive. I said a short prayer for Willa just after I got in my car and was alone. I started the engine, worked my way out of the parking garage into city traffic, accessed the interstate, arrived at home, and ate a quick lunch.

The remainder of the day passed slowly, as if the gravitational forces near a black hole had slowed time. In the midafternoon, I wanted to get some flowers for Willa, but as I drove to the florists, I realized I couldn't take flowers into the ICU, so I turned around and went back home. As I got out of the car I thought plastic or silk flowers would work instead of the real ones; the imitations would be odorless. I walked the short distance to the dollar store and bought a bouquet of artificial flowers and a get-well card. I'd take them with me in the morning.

Back at home, I sat down at the dining room table and made a list of things to talk about with Willa. I had so many questions about her life during the last thirty years. I wondered if she had kept track of me while I remained at Ocean Vista. After dinner, I tried to watch TV, but it became just noise. I couldn't get Willa out of my mind and didn't want to. I wanted to be able to cheer her up, so I imagined what she would say about having a bald head. I was going to tell her that she still looked beautiful wearing a turban. I hoped that would get a laugh. If that didn't work, I would tell her that my bald spot had been functioning fine for many years. My hair wasn't going to return and I envied her because hers would come back.

I fell asleep for about an hour and then watched the late news in a kind of stupor. At midnight I turned the set off, not remembering anything I had watched. I sat and stared at the black screen for a few minutes thinking about the new day. I had done all I could to prepare for visiting Willa in a few hours. I checked my wallet. I had enough money for lunch and dinner away from home without having to visit my bank or an ATM. I had forgotten about my credit cards, I usually paid cash for everything.

Morning came too soon. I ate a good breakfast so I wouldn't have to buy anything to eat from a machine. I was careful to avoid any aftershave and started toward the hospital at 7:30. Traffic was light on Glisan and I exceeded the speed limit by five-to-ten miles per hour. If I were pulled over, I had a good excuse. I figured a cop would understand my urgency; if not, I would pay the fine. No big deal, it would have been worth it.

I didn't see any police cars on my trip to the hospital. At the nurses' station on the fifth floor, they asked if I had a cell phone. I didn't. One of the nurses recognized me from the day before and escorted me to Willa's room.

When Willa saw me, she smiled and reached out. I felt like I wanted to sprint to her, but it was only a couple of yards distance. I walked to her slowly and said, "Good morning! Are you feeling better today?"

"Oh, Ned, I'm so happy you came back. I'm feeling pretty good, but my head still hurts a bit. The nurse gave me a pill to lessen the pain, but it makes me drowsy. How do you like my hat?" She grinned, looked up at me, and rotated her head so I could see most of her bandage.

"You look great—ready for the Easter parade—with snow on your head, or is that an eggshell?" We both laughed. "I brought you some fake flowers; they wouldn't let me bring in real ones." She took the flowers and put them in her empty plastic water glass.

"Thank you!" she gave me a great smile. Even with the bandaged head, I thought she was gorgeous.

She patted the bed and said, "Come sit beside me. I have something to tell you." Willa looked at the nurse and asked, "Could you please put the bed rail down?"

Trish lowered the side guard rail and I sat beside Willa and held her hand.

"Remember the day you came to see me and I told you to go away?"

I nodded, "I remember. I hated to hear those words. I cried like a baby all the way to Ocean Vista."

"I'm so sorry, but I was afraid if Steve saw you he would kill you. He figured out I had been seeing someone. Peggy asked me about you, so he knew something was going on. He questioned me and I just said you were my teacher and I took Peggy to your office several times."

I nodded again. "That was smart thinking—and true."

"I was really afraid for you, so I had to get you out of there. If he had come home…"

"I drove away and had to stop along the road. The tears were obscuring my lenses so I couldn't see to drive. It took a few minutes before I drove on home."

"Ned, I've always loved you, but things didn't work out the way I had planned. When I got back to Delight, I filed for a divorce and was living with my mom. When the divorce was final, I sent you a valentine, but you never wrote back. I was so disappointed."

"I got the card, Willa, but the return address was so smudged, I couldn't read it. I had thrown away all the things of yours I had from class and lab. I thought you had just been using me. I hated you for a while, for most of a year. It took me some time, but I figured you had told me to go for a good reason. When you didn't come to say goodbye, I found your Del Mar phone number and called your husband. I told him I needed your address or phone number so I could send your papers to you. I just wanted to talk to you about how I felt. He said he didn't know where you were."

Willa shook her head, gnashing her teeth, "He was lying. He knew where I was because of Peggy. He had to send child support. The day you came over, he threatened me. One of my neighbors must have told him your car was there earlier. I think I know who told him. There was an old lady living down the street and she watched what everyone in the neighborhood did. She was a busybody. He said if I got in touch with you, he'd make me watch him kill Peggy and then kill me. Then he'd dump our bodies in the mountains. We would probably never be found. Then he'd come after you."

"I'm sorry you had to go through all that, Willa. If I'd known that would happen, I would never have pursued our relationship except as a student and teacher in the classroom. I made a huge mistake. But I'm glad I fell in love with you. I've thought of you often over the years. I thought I'd never see you again."

"Ned, I wanted the relationship, but not the way it turned out. I'm glad we're together now. As soon as I get out of here, we can plan our future. What do you think?"

"That's the best idea I've heard in thirty years." I leaned over her and we kissed.

She leaned back and held my hand. "Let's talk about something that's not so gloomy, okay?"

"Okay, I'll tell you about my house. I paid off the mortgage and I've been renovating for a long time, but there are things we can do together. You can choose the paint colors—and help me paint."

"Is your house big? I've always imagined you lived in a big house."

"It's a split level, about 1,800 square feet: four bedrooms, three baths, a wood shop, and a good sized deck—on about a quarter acre. I've got three trees, lots of weeds, and about a dozen big rocks along the parking."

"Oh, I want to see it. I wonder when I'll get out of here."

Another nurse, Sally, came in and announced, "The forest service has found your car, September. It's registered to September Walker. Is Walker your last name?"

She nodded and replied, "Yes. That's my maiden name. I went back to it when my second husband passed away."

Sally continued, "The car was totaled. Your belongings were removed by the rescue service and the wreck is being stored temporarily by the forest service. Maybe Mr. Curtis can pick up your things."

I nodded. "Sure, I'll do that. I've got plenty of storage space at my home." I looked at Willa and said, "You can keep your things permanently at my place."

She smiled and opened her eyes wide, "Sounds good to me."

We talked until the nurses forced me to leave for an hour as they had done the day before. I went to the cafeteria and had a cup of free coffee. As I sat there thinking of us being together again, a state trooper approached and asked if I was Dr. Curtis.

"Yes, I'm Ned Curtis. What can I do for you?"

"I'm State Trooper Ron Watson." We shook hands and I asked him to join me. He already had a Styrofoam cup of coffee and began adding a packet of cream to it after he sat down. "The lady that was driving the white Subaru—you know if she's stable mentally?"

"I've been talking with her and she seems fine to me. I've known her for a long time. Why would you ask that?"

"The forest service asked me to investigate the accident. After all we've come up with—well, we don't think it was an accident. We believe someone forced her off the road."

"Really?"

Trooper Watson nodded. "Do you have any idea who might want her dead?"

I took a sip of coffee. "No, not the slightest. Have you talked with her?"

"The nurse told me not to. Miss Walker is in kind of a fragile mental state. They don't want to upset her. I thought you might be able to point me in the right direction for my investigation."

I shook my head, "Sorry, but I haven't seen the woman in about thirty years. I wouldn't know if she has any enemies. But if she has any, surely they would be males, maybe her first husband. I think he was a real SOB."

"Yeah. I saw her in the ICU. She's a looker all right. Probably would have been a man, but we can't rule out a woman either. Some people hold grudges for a lifetime."

The trooper got up, thanked me for my time and tossed his cup in the trash as he left the cafeteria. I sat there a little stunned with what the trooper had said. I couldn't imagine anyone trying to kill Willa, male or female. I wanted to get her out of the hospital as soon as possible so we could disappear. If someone is after her, they already know where she is. The TV broadcast guaranteed that. I'm going to stay near her as much as I can.

The hour away from Willa had expired, so I started up the stairs. After what the trooper said, I didn't want to broach the subject with Willa; I couldn't. I was the last person on earth to want to risk hurting her, especially after so recently being reunited. We had to make more plans to follow after her discharge from the hospital.

I entered the ICU with minimal scrutiny. Apparently all the nurses knew who I was, although I didn't recognize some of them. Willa was leaning against a stack of pillows and thumbing through a magazine when I entered her room. She dropped what she was reading and extended both arms toward me. I leaned over her and gave her a hug. Her head bandage had been changed and she had applied some lip gloss. She looked radiant—like she had in class many years ago.

"Boy, you look fantastic! How are you feeling?"

"I'm still a little tired, but seeing you makes me feel stronger."

Her smile was more potent than words. The changes in Willa from a day ago were dramatic. I loved seeing her radiant expression.

I had to ask, "What does the doctor say about your recovery? When will you be out of here?"

Her smile faded when she answered, "She's transferring me out of the ICU—I guess that's a good thing. You'll have to ask the nurse where they're moving me. I don't know the room number, but it will be on the floor below the ICU. I guess that's the fourth floor."

"Are you able to answer some questions? I've got a few but I don't want to upset you."

"Sure, go ahead. What do you want to know?"

"Do you remember the accident?"

"Not really. I don't think there was anything wrong with the car."

"Could someone have forced you off the road?" I watched Willa reach up and hold her head for a moment, drop her hands to the bed, and say, "I don't remember anything except driving in the mountains. The smell of the forest was wonderful—so clean."

"What about when you were in the coma?"

"Oh! There was a big dog and an Indian man. I'm trying to remember his name. The dog's name was Rover, I remember that."

"Well, don't stress out about it. I'm just curious. I don't think anything that was in your mind was real."

She smiled, "Typical scientist, huh? Getting at the facts?"

"I guess so. You know, I finished that paper you helped me with and got it published. And I still have the picture you gave me at Christmas in 1987."

"Revo Hctaw! That was his name. Kind of strange, don't you think?"

"Uh-huh. Can you spell it for me?" I wrote down the name as she gave me the letters. I noticed it was 'watch over' in reverse. I smiled and looked at Willa.

"What?" She was frowning at me.

"That's watch over reversed. Your brain was working awfully hard, dear."

"I guess so. But that's about all I can come up with. The rest is very foggy."

"That's all right, don't think about it anymore. What about your daughter? Do you know if anyone has contacted her yet?"

"I don't think so. I can't remember her number, but it's in my things from the car. You can find her number that way."

CHAPTER 23

THE NURSES ordered me a meal and I ate lunch with Willa in her ICU room. She napped afterward for about an hour. While she slept, I found out where her belongings were stored and had a hospital administrator's assistant call ahead for me. Willa's things had been transferred to a police storage facility and I drove there to pick up her belongings. It took nearly ninety minutes to retrieve her things and return to the hospital. When I got back to the ICU, I found out she had been transferred to a private room on the fourth floor.

I descended the stairs one level and asked the first nurse I saw where September Walker had been transferred. Room 412 was about a third of the way down the long hallway.

Willa was watching television when I entered the room, but when she saw me, she pressed the remote and the screen went blank.

"I can't stand those reality shows. They aren't reality anyway. What garbage!"

I laughed because I felt the same way. "How about watching cartoons together?"

She slapped me on my right wrist and laughed. Willa motioned for me to sit on the bed beside her. We held hands as we talked about our lives over the last thirty years. Some of the information was a repeat of things we had mentioned before, but much was new. We talked for at least an hour before we both fell asleep.

I woke up before Willa did and moved to a chair beside her bed. I watched her relaxed breathing and hoped she would be coming home with me before long. Nurse Doreen entered the room to check on Willa and I asked her, "Do you have any idea when September will be able to leave the hospital?"

"I'm sorry, Mr. Curtis, but the doctor hasn't commented about it. Miss Walker's vitals are not what the doctor would like to see. There are some irregularities. I think it will take a few more days."

"Do you think she's out of trouble?"

"I don't know, sir. I hope we'll have good news in a few days. Be patient, brain injuries take time to heal. Your presence seems to be helping though."

I thanked the nurse and resumed my position on the bed next to Willa. When I touched her hand, she stirred and opened her eyes.

"Ned! You're still here? Isn't it getting late?"

"It's only about 4:30. I'll start home in an hour or so. I found Peggy's number. Do you want to call her?"

Willa thought for what seemed a minute and said, "No—could you do that for me and tell her what happened? I'm not sure I can explain everything to her. She'll cry about it, too. She might want to come out here to see me, but I don't want her to do that. Tell her I will be all right and will call her as soon as I feel a little better. Okay?"

"Sure, I'll get in touch with her tonight. I'll call her as soon as I get home. That will make it about eight o'clock in Waco. Do you think the kids will be in bed?"

"Probably. After she does the dishes, she usually reads to them until they're asleep. Then she and her husband have some alone time."

"I'll wait until 8:00 central time before I call."

Willa thought for a few seconds and then said, "Okay. Tell me some more about your house and the neighborhood where you live. Do you have nice neighbors?"

We talked for another hour before we said goodbyes for the night. I leaned over her and gave her a hug and we kissed. As I backed away and waved, I could see tears cascading down her cheeks. She was reaching for a tissue as I turned and started toward the elevators. Her tears brought about some of my own. Before I pressed the down button at the elevators, I wiped my eyes. As I descended to the first floor, I wondered why Willa was exhibiting such emotion, it seemed a little out of character. Maybe the brain injury was the cause.

On the way home, I tried to construct what I would say to Peggy, remembering Willa's instructions. It was going to be interesting to talk with Peg, the last time we talked she was four years old. I imagined how her voice would sound as an adult.

After dinner, I listened to some orchestral music for a few minutes, then turned it off and sat in silence. I tried to organize my thoughts and even made a few notes. At 6:00 I dialed Peg's number. After three rings, she answered, "Hello."

"Is this Peggy?"

"Yes. Who's calling?"

"I don't think you remember me, but I'm Dr. Ned Curtis. Your mom brought you to my office several times when you were four years old. That was when you lived in Del Mar, California. You and I hunted for shells and pretty stones on the beach while your mom went swimming."

"I'm sorry, but I don't remember you." She paused, "My mother isn't here."

"Yes, I know that. She asked me to call you. She's in a hospital in Portland, Oregon."

"What? She's in the hospital? What happened? Is she all right?"

"She went off the road in the mountains and hit her head. She was in a coma for about four days. I've been with her for two days now. She asked me to call you and say that she is getting better and she will call you soon. She told me to tell you to stay home. You can't help her here. As soon as she gets out of the hospital, she will live with me. We've always wanted to be together. It's been a long time and we thought it would never happen."

"What's your name again?"

"Ned. Ned Curtis."

"Oh! I do remember. You're Dr. Ned. You had the colored tinker toys that I played with on the floor."

"You're right! That was a long time ago. I wish I could see you now. I'll bet you are a gorgeous young woman."

Peg laughed, "Ha! Not after having two kids. Things have sagged due to gravity and having children. I'm more like an old pair of shoes, comfortable, but difficult to shine."

We both laughed.

"You have a good sense of humor, Peg. As soon as your mother gets well and we get organized, we'll come visit you. I'd like to meet your husband and see the kids."

"It would be like meeting you for the first time—it was so long ago; I only have vague notions of you. But you have a very nice voice."

"Thank you. You sound younger than you are. I'd guess you were in your twenties from the sound of your voice. Well, I'd better let you go. Sorry that I had to give you some bad news, but we'll hope for the best."

"Thank you for the call, Ned. Tell Mom hi for me."

"I'll do that in the morning. Goodbye, Peg."

"Bye, Dr. Ned." I could hear her smile when she said Dr. Ned.

I sat and thought about our conversation for a few minutes before I got a cup of decaf and turned on the TV.

September woke up to a knocking at the cabin door. She folded back the covers, wiped the sleep from her eyes, and slipped into a robe. She was wearing socks so didn't bother with slippers. She couldn't even see her house shoes; she had kicked them under the bed when she last removed them.

"Just a minute. I'm coming." Who could be at the door so early in the morning?

She swung the door open and saw Revo. He had a big, larger than life, smile. September suspected he wanted more cookies.

"Revo! Come in. I didn't think I would see you again. You said you were going away."

"It's good to see you, September. My return was unexpected. I didn't think I would be back so soon." Revo entered the room and sat down on the sofa. His clothes were not rumpled as before, they were pressed and his black shoes were polished to a brilliant shine. They would have easily passed a rigorous military inspection.

"Would you like a cookie? I think I still have some."

"No, thank you. I would like you to come with me. I found a beautiful meadow that I think you should see. You will be pleased with the tranquility and magnificence of the landscape. The flowers are of such beauty! The sky is so blue and so clear you can see forever."

"Oh! You have to show me. Let me put on some shoes." She turned toward the bedroom. "Is it far?"

"Not far. You'll be surprised that you didn't see it sooner."

September dressed in white jeans, a white cotton blouse, laced up her athletic shoes, and rejoined Revo.

"I'm ready. Let's go! I'm anxious to see this place. Should I lock the door? Will we be gone long?"

"You can lock the door if you like. It won't matter."

Revo led the way into the forest. They walked for about five minutes before a clearing appeared. A couple was walking toward them through the luxurious green grass and beautiful flowers of all shapes, colors and sizes. When the couple was about ten yards distant, September recognized her mother and father. She ran toward them, arms outstretched.

"Mom! Dad!"

They replied, "Willa! It is so good to see you. We are a family again!"

Revo addressed the family, "I will go now. There are others to see and messages to deliver." He looked directly at September and said, "Enjoy your forever life, Willa."

I had gone to bed late and was sleeping soundly when the phone rang. I answered on the fourth ring.

"Hello. Yes, this is Ned Curtis."

"I'm a social worker at Portland NE Hospital. Were you visiting with Miss September Walker starting two days ago"

"Yes. How is she doing today? Is she being discharged?"

"I'm sorry to have to tell you this, Mr. Curtis, but Miss Walker passed away early this morning. She had a massive stroke and we couldn't save her. The doctors did everything possible. Could you please notify her daughter? We don't have any contact information."

I could barely speak, but I was able to choke out Peggy's phone number. I dropped the phone into its cradle, sat down on the sofa, and began to cry. I must have wept for ten minutes before I began to regain control of my emotions. After thirty years of being separated and then finally getting back together, Willa was taken from me, this time forever. All of our plans had vanished in an instant. Those thirty years of doubt had been erased in one day of conversation and then our few hours of planning for the future had vanished as a result of a few words spoken over a phone.

I had no options. I couldn't bear to see her lifeless form. We hadn't considered death; we had only thought of our future days together. Everything was gone. I wondered if we were being punished for violating one of the Ten Commandments, but if that were true then I would be taken, too. But perhaps I was being punished; Willa had been taken from me a final time. I sat there and began to forget about my feelings and had to consider those of Peg. How was Peggy going to take the news? If she travelled to Portland, I would support her in any way I could.

I paced through rooms of the house for a time before I came to my senses. I made some coffee and sat at the kitchen table thinking of September. I recalled our times together thirty years ago and those recent seemingly brief moments. However, the thoughts were short lived. I began to feel as if I were destined to have lonely years and grow very old with thoughts that might have been. Although I am approaching the December of my life, I will always remember the good times September and I had and our rekindled love.